"Cover me."

The demand was shouted over sizzling gunfire as Rafael Encizo raced toward the stairway.

Gary Manning responded to his partner's request by letting his .357 Eagle rip into a flesh-and-blood target like a hungry Magnum piranha.

Encizo glanced back down the steps to assure himself that Manning was safe. The Cuban returned his gaze to the top of the steps and looked directly into the barrel of a Beretta 92SB. The Phoenix warrior stopped and swung his MP-5 into play, although his mind had already registered the fact that it was too late.

The Beretta fired.

Lightning streaked against Encizo's skull. Something warm washed over his eyes. The weight of his H&K machine gun dragged him down. The Cuban felt the strength in his legs slip away, and then he was falling.

Rafael Encizo fell headfirst down the shaft of a dark, bottomless pit.

Mack Bolan's
PHOENIX FORCE

PHOENIX FORCE

The Twisted Cross

Gar Wilson

A GOLD EAGLE BOOK FROM
WORLDWIDE

TORONTO • NEW YORK • LONDON • PARIS
AMSTERDAM • STOCKHOLM • HAMBURG
ATHENS • MILAN • TOKYO • SYDNEY

First edition January 1986

ISBN 0-373-61321-0

Special thanks and acknowledgment to Paul Glen Neuman
and William Fieldhouse for their contributions to this work.

Printed in Canada

1

Jean-Paul Albert had a migraine.

The young Frenchman blinked his eyes and tried to ignore the rising tide of pain creeping across the front of his head, but it was useless. His vision became more blurred with each passing second as he steered his Volkswagen bus through the congestion of Friday night traffic along the Avenue des Champs Elysees.

At another time and place, Albert would have found somewhere to park to wait out the headache. At another time and place the consequences of getting one of his migraines would have amounted to an annoying inconvenience he could live with. Tonight, however, he did not have that luxury. Tonight he had a mission to complete; the most important undertaking of his entire life.

Keeping his VW on course, Albert reached his free hand into his coat pocket and withdrew the large bottle of aspirin he always carried. Holding the bottle in his fist, he popped off its cap with his thumb, then tilted the bottle to his lips and filled his mouth with more than a dozen of the bitter-tasting pills.

He discarded the half-empty bottle and chewed the aspirin, grinding the pills to chalky powder before swallowing them in a single raspy gulp. Albert squeezed his eyes shut, then opened them again. That was better. In a couple of minutes the reverberating pain inside his head would begin to diminish.

Traffic slowed as the young Frenchman approached the Place de la Concorde, the impressive square that had served as an executioner's playground during the French Revolution. It was here that Louis XVI and his queen, Marie-Antoinette, had lost their heads to the guillotine.

A 3,000-year-old Egyptian obelisk had long since replaced the guillotine as the square's centerpiece. But Albert thought it would have made more sense to have left the efficient killing machine intact. With Madame Guillotine on the job once more, Albert had no doubt that France could reclaim the glory of its illustrious past.

Albert concentrated on the lights of the wrought-iron lampposts surrounding the square and noted that already the aspirin seemed to be working. The sharp pain from his migraine was gradually giving way to a dull pulsating throb. He rolled down his window and took a deep breath of the chill winter air. The shock of the change in temperature caused his teeth to chatter.

He closed the window and checked the time on his watch. Fifteen minutes to go before the broadcast. No problem. Even if he continued at his present speed, he would still arrive at the Louvre long before the ceremony began.

The traffic surged forward and Albert eased his foot down on the VW's accelerator. He sped by an eighteenth-century palace that now served as the Navy Ministry and then past the American embassy.

Damned Americans, the young Frenchman thought. If not for the United States and its meddling interference, he would still be at home in the south of France, far from the corruption and greed that was Paris.

Albert directed his Volkswagen toward his ultimate destination. Sprawled in the heart of Paris, the Louvre is home to one of the finest collections of art in the world. Albert disagreed. He believed the famous museum served as a stinging reminder that the French government hoarded its wealth in the north, failing to share its riches with the south.

Such shameless thievery had to be stopped, and it was up to dedicated men, true patriots like him, to see that it was. Life without equality was not worth living. Earning that equality was something worth dying for.

Albert crossed the Seine, looking for a place to park, pulled his VW up over the curb and brought the bus to a halt. He shut off the engine and climbed outside, leaving the keys in the ignition. If someone wanted to steal the Volkswagen before the police discovered it, that was fine by him.

Raising the collar of his woolen coat to protect himself from the icy wind blowing off the Seine, Albert headed for the Louvre. He counted each step as he went. When he reached sixty-three he came to the Quai des Tuileries, and boldly walked into the street.

Brakes screeched and automobile horns blared as motorists did their best to avoid running him over. Somehow he did not get hit.

"Qu'est-ce que vous foutez là?" an angry voice shouted, but Albert was oblivious to the annoyed driver's wrath.

Albert's heart pounded with excitement. He shook his head. The steady throbbing behind his eyes was getting worse. So much for the aspirin; his migraine was returning. Already miniature fireworks were going off inside his skull. Albert knew he had to hurry. Once a migraine locked onto his brain, it would be hours before he would be good for anything.

The ticket windows at the entrance to the Louvre were closed for the evening—not too surprising since the broadcast of the ceremony was to take place in the open air rather than inside the museum.

The Frenchman had expected to encounter museum guards by now, but he entered the Louvre's courtyard unchallenged. He immediately saw that the area where the ceremony was to take place had been cordoned off to prevent any unauthorized intruders from disrupting the proceedings. All who entered had to pass through a security check not far from where he stood. Two uniformed guards, gendarmes of the Paris police department, were in charge of this function. Both men were attired in the dark blue ceremonial dress of the *Garde Republicaine de Paris*.

Albert clenched his teeth and slowed his pace as more of the fireworks exploded in his head. When he reached the security checkpoint one of the guards requested his identification. He complied by presenting a laminated card from his coat pocket.

The card was genuine—it identified him as a reporter for the newspaper *Le Figaro*—but the name stamped on it belonged to a man who had died upholding the honor of France during World War I.

Albert waited while the second policeman checked the name against a master list. The list was three sheets long, and when the officer failed to locate the name on the first page, Albert became tense. Had he been betrayed? He had been assured that getting through the security check would not be a problem.

Cold sweat glistened on his brow. All would be lost if the gendarmes saw through his ruse. He would be arrested and the ceremony would continue as scheduled. His mind was preparing to offer some excuse about why his name did not appear on the list, when the policeman checking the names smiled.

Albert breathed a sigh of relief.

"Merci," the officer said, returning the press card as he and his colleague moved aside to permit the young Frenchman to enter the restricted area.

Albert nodded in response and pocketed the card. The half-witted police had let him through, and without even checking for concealed weapons. In spite of the terrible migraine raging in his head, Albert grinned.

If the idiot gendarmes survived this night they would never again be assigned to a position of responsibility. And if the two *flic* fools were killed, then that was their hard luck. Either way, after tonight their careers in law enforcement were finished.

A stage was erected opposite the Louvre's principal entrance, directly in front of the impressive equestrian statue that depicted the Marquis de Lafayette in all his glory. The statue had been a gift to France by a group of school children from the United States. The location of the stage was no accident; Lafayette represented a historic highlight in Franco-American relations.

Albert estimated that two hundred spectators were already on hand to view the event. French television crews, plus those from the United States, Great Britain and Germany all vied for the best vantage point from which to cover the show.

Banks of spotlights bathed the surface of the stage in a solid sheet of bright white light. A streamer of alternating French and American flags was draped overhead. It was enough to turn Albert's stomach.

Pushing through the audience, Albert soon found himself standing behind a BBC news team whose cameras were trained on the podium positioned in the center of the stage. A firecracker went off, and Albert's body jerked in surprise. He turned to see where the noise had come from, before realizing the painful truth.

The cherry bomb was another symptom of his migraine's growing strength. His fingers opened the bottom button of his coat. A glance at his watch showed the ceremony was already running a few minutes late. He massaged his temples with his thumbs. Another firecracker went off.

From behind the stage a brass band began to play. The music was from a march Albert remembered hearing as a child. Sticks beat solidly upon drums. A whistle blew and the musicians paraded onto the stage. Albert coughed and pressed his temples harder with his thumbs. At long last the program was beginning.

As the Frenchman watched, the members of the band split into two groups, each group marching to opposite sides of the stage. Albert counted twenty musicians altogether. They marched into place, and then with a flurry of drums, the piece was over. The musicians lowered their instruments as the enthusiastic audience responded with applause. The noise did nothing to help Albert's migraine.

The audience was still applauding wildly when three men appeared and took their place behind the podium. Albert saw his targets come into view.

First was Richard Poussin, the Vice-President of France. Poussin was in his late fifties and had a pot belly. Albert knew Poussin's physique typified the gluttony so prevalent in the north.

Next came General Georges Goulinat, French army hero and something of a media favorite with Parisians. Goulinat had distinguished himself in numerous battle campaigns during the Second World War. Nearly seventy, the physically fit general had retired with full military honors.

None of this impressed Albert. As far as he was concerned, General Georges Goulinat was a traitor to his people. Born in the south in the tiny village of Limoux, Goulinat had shunned his true homeland when he retired. Instead of returning to live out his years in Limoux, Goulinat had chosen to stay in Paris. He'd traded his birthright for the pampered riches of the north. A man like Georges Goulinat did not deserve to live.

Last onto the stage was an American Air Force colonel named E. J. Bidnik. The press had reported that Colonel Bidnik was one of nine United States Air Force and Army officers selected to spearhead the new American invasion of France. By actively participating in the evening's celebration, Bidnik had condemned himself to death.

Albert frowned. He was confused. He had been coached to expect four dignitaries at the broadcast. Yet only three had appeared. Should he wait, he wondered? But, no. It was now or never.

With all eyes focused on the stage Albert made his move. Going to the right, he gingerly stepped over the cables running to the BBC equipment. The pressure inside his head was intolerable. He dropped his fingers to the front of his coat and popped open two more buttons. His mouth felt as dry as a bucket of sand.

The audience was still applauding when he reached the area where the German television crew was filming. No one paid him the slightest bit of attention as he continued toward the short metal stairway that led to the stage. The applause was beginning to fade.

Albert fed his right hand into his coat pocket and withdrew what resembled a black cigarette case. In the center of the case was a white plastic switch. Only a handful of the audience was applauding now. It was time for him to act, to end the ceremony before a single word of the treasonous celebration could be broadcast to the world.

Throwing open the final button of his coat, Albert rushed up the stairs to the stage. Several members of the brass marching band glanced in his direction. A security guard appeared and caught him by the back of his coat. Albert shrugged and felt the coat pull away from his body. Then he was free and running toward the podium.

Someone in the audience screamed, and Albert ran faster. Vice-President Poussin turned and emitted a high-pitched squeal like the fat pig he was. Albert shoved Poussin aside and out of the way. General Goulinat and Colonel Bidnik moved toward the intruder but backed off quickly once they saw Albert's vest and the detonator box he held in his hand.

Albert stood at the podium, facing the audience. It was exactly where he wanted to be: the center of attention. The migraine blurred his vision. He extended his right arm, holding the detonator in his hand for everyone to see, and then shouted into the bank of microphones.

"La France dirigée par les français...pas les américains!" Albert proclaimed for all the world to hear. "A France ruled by France...not the Americans!"

Albert ran his thumb over the white plastic switch on the detonator and snapped it forward. A blinding flash of light transformed night into day.

Jean-Paul Albert lost his migraine.

2

The terrorist charged to the middle of the stage and shoved the French vice-president out of his way. The killer raised his right arm in a gesture of defiance and shouted out his message. Then he smiled and detonated the bomb he was wearing. All color vanished from the screen as the terrorist went nova on the monitor.

The video transmission did a jump cut, and an off-camera announcer indicated that the explosion had occurred fifteen minutes earlier. Only a pile of broken rubble suggested that there had been a stage in front of the pedestal of jagged stone, which was all that remained of the LaFayette monument. Much of the wreckage was comprised of blasted bodies and severed limbs. The spotlights that once highlighted the band now reflected off the brass fragments of shattered musical instruments.

Medics scoured the site of the attack, searching for survivors, but as they sifted through the debris the death toll rose steadily. Police combed the area for clues. Bits of multicolored fabric—tiny strips of cloth from the banner of French and American flags—decorated the courtyard like confetti.

The camera did an about-face and surveyed the extent of the damage sustained by the audience. The grim picture was much the same. Bodies littered the ground in various poses of death. Medical teams did their best to save the lives of the wounded. Ambulances in the background were filled to capacity.

Scattered survivors stumbled about in shock. One victim of the ruthless assault clutched his hands to his chest and collapsed. Another cried softly as she cradled the head of a dead man in her lap. The camera moved in close for a tight shot of the woman's tear-streaked face. Then the monitor screen went blank.

"Bloody diabolical," David McCarter summed up his review of the video as the lights in the War Room of Stony Man headquarters came back on. "What the hell are the bastards behind that massacre going to do for an encore?"

"Let's hope they don't get the chance," Hal Brognola commented, easing back in his chair and putting a flame to the end of the cigar lodged in the corner of his mouth. "A full season of shows like this one is more than I want to know about."

"You and the rest of us," McCarter assured Brognola.

Hal Brognola nodded. As the nation's top federal agent and liaison between the White House and all Stony Man missions, he was well aware that the five men sitting before him would have done everything humanly possible to prevent the attack at the Louvre. Unfortunately it often took such tragedies to pinpoint precisely where Brognola's band of crack anti-terrorists were needed most.

Given the nature of the cold-blooded attack in Paris, putting the Phoenix Force superpros to work in France was Brognola's top priority. Those responsible for the massacre had to be located and stopped before they could kill again. Brognola could think of no group better suited to that task than the battle-hardened men of Phoenix Force.

Stony Man had originally been created for the sole purpose of tapping into the unique crime-fighting talents of Mack Bolan. Known to both law-enforcement agencies and his enemies as the Executioner, Bolan had waged a relentless one-man war against the seemingly insurmountable might of the Mafia.

Through the hell and horror of thirty-eight campaigns Bolan had hammered away at the Mafia's foundations, dealing with the dons of the Black Hand in a manner the lords of organized crime understood all too well. The Mafia was a cancer voraciously devouring the lifeblood of the nation, a sickness whose growth had progressed unchecked for too many years.

The Executioner had other ideas. Business as usual for the Mafia soon became a thing of the past. Bolan introduced a new word to the dons' vocabulary, and that word was fear. Bolan gave the Mafia a taste of its own medicine and watched in satisfaction as the czars of crime and their followers perished from an overdose of overdue justice.

When the final battle was finished the families of the once-powerful dons had all but been destroyed. At long last the Executioner's war was over.

Bolan barely had time to consider his options for the future, when a decision was made for him. Called upon by the President of the United States to wage a new war against the rising tide of international terrorism, the Executioner was faced with a proposal he was conscience-bound to accept.

And so the Stony Man project was launched. The U.S. government listed the Executioner as officially killed in action, and Mack Bolan was reborn in the guise of Colonel John Phoenix. Two professional teams of antiterrorists were created to assist him: Able Team and Phoenix Force.

The decision to have Hal Brognola direct the Stony Man program was an easy one. During Bolan's hotly contested war with the Mafia, Brognola had secretly aided the Executioner in his fight. Brognola jumped at the opportunity to work alongside Bolan again.

The Stony Man project was a winner from the start. In one decisive confrontation after another, terrorists worldwide paid for their crimes against humanity with their lives. Stony Man seemed to be operating on a roll of unending victories, an unblemished rate of success unparalleled in the annals of antiterrorism.

Then the growing list of foes retaliated, assaulting Stony Man headquarters in an attack that claimed the lives of April Rose and Stony Man's weapons expert, Andrej Konzaki.

Stony Man's troubles did not end there. A carefully orchestrated plot forced Mack Bolan to relinquish all ties to Stony Man and the United States. "Colonel Phoenix" was labeled a cold-blooded killer and became a criminal sought by every major law-enforcement agency in the world.

During Stony Man's dark days Hal Brognola's unwavering faith in Phoenix Force and Able Team kept the organization afloat. In the end, Brognola's trust in his men was more than vindicated. Stony Man had proved itself time and again, and now with the massacre in Paris thrust upon them, his Phoenix commandos would be called upon once more to do the impossible.

Phoenix Force was the new Foreign Legion—five who fought like five hundred. Five fearless soldiers who could accomplish what the strength of governments could not.

"As soon as we receive clearance from the White House," Brognola said, "you're on your way to France."

"Any takers claiming responsibility for the attack?" McCarter asked.

Brognola shook his head.

David McCarter's bio read like a who's who of the world of antiterrorism. Raised in one of the rougher sections of London's East End, the stubborn Cockney was a veteran of Great Britain's Special Air Service.

A former national champion of the British Pistol Marksmanship Team, McCarter excelled in practically every form of combat. He was also an excellent pilot. Prior to joining Phoenix Force, he had seen action in Southeast Asia, locked horns with Communist subversives during an undercover stint in Hong Kong, served in Oman at the time of the Omani Ohofar War and participated in the SAS assault on the Iranian Embassy in London.

"Usually the media have been contacted by now," Brognola admitted. "But so far the crazies behind the hit are laying low."

"Considering the reputation France enjoys as a haven for terrorists," Gary Manning offered, "we could be talking about any number of left-wing organizations. I'm not too surprised. The French government shouldn't be, either. You haul enough shit through the middle of town and some of it's bound to fall off the back of the truck."

The Phoenix team's top sniper, Gary Manning, was also one of the world's foremost authorities on explosives and demolition. Manning had served as a lieutenant in the Canadian army, and saw action in Vietnam with a hush-hush Special Operations Group in which his superior skills as a demo man were much in demand. The barrel-chested Canadian was one of a handful of his countrymen to receive the Silver Star for valor from the United States during the Vietnam conflict.

After Nam, Gary Manning's thirst for adventure led him to join the Royal Canadian Mounted Police. He soon found a home in the RCMP's antiterrorist division, and was eventually posted to Europe, where he worked with the famed GSG-9 antiterrorists of West Germany.

Shortly afterward, the RCMP's role in espionage was brought to a halt. The demise of Manning's unit basically left the Canadian workaholic out in the cold. He was offered a desk job by the newly formed Canadian Security Intelligence Service, but he turned it down, rightly reasoning that the life of a nine-to-five paper pusher was not for him.

Manning opted for two major changes in his life. He entered the private sector and he decided to settle down and raise a family. All he really raised was his blood pressure. The marriage went sour, but the big Canadian did not mourn its passing. He was working as a security consultant for North American International when cast as a founding member of Phoenix Force.

"What's the initial death toll?" Rafael Encizo asked. "It has to be high."

"Too high," Brognola said, confirming the Cuban's suspicions. "Everyone on the stage was killed. Including the madman responsible for the destruction, that means twenty-five dead. We still don't know how many people in the audience lost their lives. All the television crews covering the event suffered fatalities. There probably won't be an exact death toll available for at least a couple of days, and perhaps not even then. Some of the bodies on the stage and nearby were so badly mutilated they're beyond recognition or identification."

"Which has to go double for the terrorist's body," Encizo concluded.

"You got it," Brognola said. "There wasn't enough left of him to stick on the back of a stamp."

"It's a shame there wasn't time to gun the *cagado* down before he threw the switch," the Cuban mused. "A damn shame."

A verteran of the Bay of Pigs invasion in 1961, Rafael Encizo was taken prisoner by the Communists and dumped in El Principe, the hellhole of a prison featuring exclusive accommodations for Castro's political opponents. Subjected to the sadistic whims of Russian "technicians," whose behavior-modification techniques included a healthy diet of daily beatings and little food, the stocky Cuban endured his tormentor's vicious hospitality until the day he broke his guard's neck and managed to escape.

Back in the States, Encizo made a living in a variety of occupations: he was a scuba instructor, treasure hunter and professional bodyguard. Along the way he became a naturalized citizen. His last job prior to joining Stony Man's Phoenix Force was as an insurance investigator specializing in maritime claims.

"It's quite possible we may never learn the terrorist's identity," Brognola stated as he exhaled a cloud of cigar smoke.

"Especially if whoever put the scum up to the deed keeps mum about it," McCarter added. "Why the hell go through all the agro to get everyone's attention and then not claim the glory? That makes as much sense as writing your last will and testament and then refusing to sign it."

"No one ever accused these savages of being sensible," Manning countered. "If they were they'd be in some other line of work."

"That's right." Calvin James agreed. "But the bad news is that some of these creeps want to make slaughtering innocent bystanders a full-time job. They'd welcome a sixty-hour work week if it meant washing their hands in the blood of their victims at the end of each shift.

"For my money," the Force's black commando continued, "I don't get any comfort knowing that the cruds behind the attack haven't come forward. By now they should have made their silly statement to the press, then moved on to plan their next party. Maybe they haven't done this because the hit at the Louvre was only the first course of a much larger meal. If that's the case, we've only seen the tip of the iceberg, and that scares me."

Calvin James did not frighten easily. Growing up in the slums of Chicago's tough south side had taken care of that. In his neighborhood, where making it in one piece from sunrise to sunset was considered a major victory, Calvin James had been a natural survivor. Although he was only seventeen when he enlisted in the Navy, James was already battle-hardened pro.

Trained as a hospital corpsman, James excelled in his studies and soon gained the attention of the SEALS. His expertise led to a special assignment in which he traded the concrete jungles of the United States for the genuine greenery of Vietnam.

His tour of duty ended two years later when James was wounded during a particularly vicious attack. He was decorated for courage and devotion in combat and returned Stateside with an honorable discharge.

Back from the Land of Ho, James continued his studies in medicine and chemistry on the GI bill. But one personal tragedy after another, including the murders of his mother and sister, convinced him to join the San Francisco Police Department. His combat skills led him straight into a position with the SFPD's Special Weapons and Tactics section.

When Phoenix Force needed a man with his talents, Calvin James's name was at the top of the list. Recruited for a one-shot stint with the Stony Man supersquad, the black commando's involvement became permanent after Keio Ohara, one of the Force's original members, died in combat on the same mission.

"Calvin's right," Colonel Yakov Katzenelenbogen said. "What happened at the Louvre could be a small whimper before the big bang. There's no mistaking the fact that the terrorist's dying statement was strongly anti-American. Maybe that's the only statement those behind the hit wanted to make. At least for now. Of course, the fanatic's final words could just as easily have been a smoke screen to throw everyone off."

"Hell of a waste of free publicity if that's true," Manning declared. "The blast is the number-one topic on every major newscast. But it wouldn't be the first time terrorists pulled some sleight-of-hand crap to hide the dirt up their sleeves."

"And it wouldn't be the first time such monsters covered their tracks in blood," Katzenelenbogen added.

Colonel Yakov Katzenelenbogen, senior member and unit commander of Phoenix Force, looked as if he would be more at home behind the counter of a flower shop. The Israeli's decidedly paunchy midsection, iron-gray hair and gentle eyes did not fit Hollywood's image of a crack antiterrorist. The only clue to Katzenelenbogen's occupation was his right arm, amputated just below the elbow.

Involved since a teenager in warfare, antiterrorism and the seamy realities of covert intelligence, Katz had fought alongside Resistance fighters against the Nazis during World War II. His skills increased with the Haganah and Israel's struggle for independence against the British, and were later honed to perfection with the Mossad.

The Six Day War cost Katz his only son and his right arm. In place of that missing arm he usually wore a three-pronged hook prosthesis. A patient man whose compassion made him a champion of the oppressed everywhere, Katz's able leadership on the battlefield had proved an invaluable asset to the Phoenix Force team.

"Maybe the massacre in Paris was a genuine terrorist reaction to the increasing American presence in France," James suggested. "I can't think of any fringe organization that would support the French government's decision to begin negotiations to reopen our U.S. military bases there. After the heavy pullout back in '66 that's the last most of them ever expected or wanted to see of us."

"France isn't throwing down the welcome mat for old time's sake," Brognola added. "The strength the Communist Party's gained since the U.S. bases closed has many of the French politicians very worried. To them we're the lesser of two evils. They figure an increased American presence will at least let them hang on to their jobs."

McCarter shrugged. "If the French government got off its collective fat arse the Communists wouldn't stand a chance. Opening the U.S. military bases again makes it easy for them. The attitude in France has always been sort of laissez-faire. They get the other bloke to do the dirty work, then bugger off to congratulate themselves over a glass of wine."

Further discussion stopped when the speaker phone on the conference table began to ring. The telephone served as an ultrasecure link with the White House.

Hal Brognola leaned forward and answered the call. "Yes, Mr. President?"

"Good evening," came the commander-in-chief's familiar voice. "I'm assuming you and our five friends have had time to review the unedited videotape that was sent over."

"That is correct, sir," Brognola replied. "All five are with me now. We've just finished watching the tape, and what we saw is very alarming."

"Without question. I've been talking to the French president for the past half hour. The whole country is in an uproar. The death toll from this tragic incident has risen past one hundred. More fatalities are expected by morning."

"And I don't imagine the terrorist's dying words are helping matters any," Brognola said.

"Not at all. Certainly we anticipated some opposition to the French government's proposal that the United States reopen its military bases there, but nothing like this was ever dreamed of."

"Then the sooner our friends get to France the better for all of us."

"My feelings exactly," the President stated. "And when they arrive they can expect full cooperation from the French DST. I've been assured that anything they require is theirs for the asking."

"Excellent, sir. Was there anything else?"

"Time is of the essence for this one. Unchecked, anti-American sentiments could effectively neutralize any hope for getting our bases back into France. Strategically, increasing our military presence in Europe is the last thing the Soviets want. They don't want France to accommodate us."

"We'll do our best to prevent that, sir."

"I don't doubt it. Air Force One is at your disposal as soon as Phoenix Force is ready."

Brognola established eye contact with Katz, then calmly reported, "They're ready now, Mr. President."

3

Adolf Zeigler sat comfortably in the high-backed leather armchair sipping his glass of *Kirschwasser*. A roaring fire blazed in the room's massive fireplace, and the cracking and popping of the burning wood nostalgically reminded the ODESSA officer of the sound of breaking bones. The noise was pleasant to his ears.

A large man with wide muscular shoulders and rough, powerful hands, Zeigler motioned for Rotten-führer Schmidt to rewind the video cassette. What a beautiful thing is victory, he thought, watching through his right eye as Schmidt hurried to carry out his order. His left eye was sightless, a milky white orb framed above and below by a livid scar that ran from his eyebrow to his cheek.

Zeigler could have hidden the blind eye beneath a patch, but did not. His feelings about the scar on his face were much the same. With the storehouse of Third Reich wealth available to him, he could easily have improved his physical appearance with the finest reconstructive surgery money could buy.

But the scar and ruined eye were a source of inspiration to his men, living symbols of proof that all who followed the cause of the Reich must be prepared to sacrifice. Zeigler wore his symbols proudly.

He drank more of his cherry brandy and allowed a satisfied smile to play upon his lips. At last the plan, *his plan*, was underway. Dreams die hard, and those of conquest even harder, but now thanks to his bold and cunning proposal, the glory of the past was to be reborn.

For more than forty years he had kept the dream alive. While others less stalwart than he had faltered, Zeigler's faith in his beliefs had remained steadfast. Rising through the ranks to become ODESSA's chief of intelligence operations, he had recently been promoted to second-in-command after a debilitating stroke disabled Otto Thiel.

Poor Thiel. Once the pride and joy of the Fatherland, he had been reduced to a paralyzed shell of his former self. The man who was once a mastermind behind ODESSA now spent his days staring blankly at the walls of his room, perpetual drool spilling over his chin.

Of course, having Thiel out of the way had its compensations. Zeigler's promotion meant he now controlled all the ODESSA agents under Thiel's command; that plus the formidable *Hauptquartier*, a base of operations high in the Pyrenees.

Zeigler once suggested to Otto Thiel that they pool their respective talents. But Thiel, the stubborn *Affenarsch*, saw the suggestion as a sign that Zeigler meant to steal his coveted position as ODESSA's second-in-command.

Otto Thiel had been correct, of course, but that did not stop Zeigler from trying. When word of his superior's stroke first reached him, Zeigler treated the news as a personal sign that it was time to implement his plan.

Otto Thiel may have been a dedicated Nazi, but he was not a man of vision. He was not an Adolf Zeigler. With his ascension up another rung of ODESSA's ladder, Zeigler had moved that much closer to what he knew in his heart was his destiny—to inherit command of the entire Nazi Party.

Each journey begins with a step, and Zeigler's began with the bomb blast at the Louvre. He still marveled at how smoothly the attack had gone, even at the hands of a Frenchman. Some things never change. Zeigler had used the same tactics during the war. Whenever he'd wanted a really dirty piece of business taken care of, he'd always given the job to a Frenchman. The avaricious idiots were cheap and eager to please.

Zeigler finished his cherry brandy and poured himself another. The only thing wrong with the business at the Louvre was that the guest list for the celebration had been incomplete. Watching the videotape had shown him that much. But Zeigler was not bothered. The insignificant problem in Paris would soon be rectified.

"Will that be all, *Herr Obergruppenführer*?" Schmidt asked as the tape of the Louvre disaster completed its rewind.

Zeigler looked up from his drink. "Play it again for me, *bitte. Ja*, Schmidt? I've waited such a long time for this production to start. Seeing our enemies finally beginning to die brings home a special kind of satisfaction. Let's view the tape again."

While Schmidt pushed the Play button on the videotape recorder, Zeigler settled back into his chair to watch the show. At sixty-five, he was the picture of health. He had never felt better. But was that so surprising? After all these years he had a reason to feel good.

At an age when most men were looking forward to retirement, Adolf Zeigler was on the verge of taking command of a country.

4

Air Force One was on the ground at Orly Airport only long enough to refuel and for the men of Phoenix Force to disembark with their gear. In the time it took to travel from the United States to Paris in the President's Boeing 707, no major breakthroughs had been made in the investigation into the terrorist attack at the Louvre.

Halfway across the Atlantic the Force had received a message from Washington via the French secret service that UCLAT, the *Unité pour la coordination de la lutte contre le terrorisme*, France's internal counterterrorist organization, had a possible lead, but no further details had been available. They would be briefed on specifics once they touched down in France.

Edmond Dupont, their UCLAT contact, was waiting for them at Orly as they stepped off the jet. Aroused to the point of frustration over the cowardly bombing at the Louvre, Dupont was further annoyed that outsiders, especially those from the United States, had been summoned to assist in UCLAT's investigation. What made the situation more intolerable for the French intelligence officer was that he had been told to take orders from them.

Dupont knew that this humiliating gesture of servility would hamper him from conducting a proper investigation. It was an insult pure and simple. The five men from the U.S. would amount to nothing more than an unwanted anchor around his neck. The last thing he needed was to baby-sit a bunch of excess baggage. Dupont's prejudicial opinion of the men he had been ordered to assist did not change as he watched the strangers descend the ramp from the American president's private jet. If anything, his antagonistic feelings grew stronger.

Mon Dieu! What kind of so-called commandos were these? One of them looked as if he should be sitting at home in front of a television set, surrounded by an army of grandchildren. In the proper light the man could have passed for an old-age pensioner. *Putain!* Was this to be believed? The elderly man with the contented stomach had only one arm. *Quelle chérie!*

"*Bon soir,*" Dupont said, popping open the trunk of his BMW for the men to stow their luggage. "I am Edmond Dupont of UCLAT," he introduced himself in English. "My instructions from my superiors are to accommodate you gentlemen in any way I can."

The tone in Dupont's voice, while cordial, told Katz all he needed to know about the French secret serviceman's true sentiments regarding the orders from his superiors. Not that Dupont's gripes mattered one way or the other. Katz had no patience for such pettiness.

The UCLAT agent appeared to be in his middle-to-late thirties and matched the description Phoenix Force had been given while en route to France. Dupont was approximately six feet tall, with narrow shoulders and the trim physique of an athlete. He wore his dark hair trimmed short and parted to the right. His eyes had a perpetual unhappy look to them, and seemed ready to brim over with tears.

Dupont's UCLAT uniform consisted of a flannel suit in a fashionable style that would not reach the clothing stores of the U.S. for another two seasons.

"Bon soir," Katz said in French, one of six languages he spoke fluently. The Israeli colonel offered his left hand, which Dupont dutifully shook. "My name is Gray," Katz said supplying his cover name. "My associates and I are eager to get to work. We were informed during our journey that UCLAT may have developed a lead for us. Can you elaborate?"

"I will be happy to," Dupond replied, "but after we are on our way into the city. If you gentlemen will kindly find seats to your liking, I will drive as we discuss the information you desire."

He slammed the trunk lid closed over their luggage, then climbed in behind the wheel of the BMW and started the engine. Katz rode up front with Dupont, while the remaining four men of the Phoenix Force squad settled down in the cramped space in the rear of the BMW. David McCarter, being the last to get in, was forced to sit sideways and on the edge of the seat. As soon as the Briton slammed his door shut, Dupont dropped the transmission into gear and they were off.

Upon landing, Air Force One had been directed to an isolated offshoot of Orly's southernmost runway. Dupont followed a two-lane road that veered away from where they had landed, and headed the BMW through a security checkpoint leading out of the airport. Dupont presented a pass to the soldier standing guard at the gate and they were promptly waved through. Seconds later Dupont had the BMW speeding north, heading toward Paris.

"So what's the story on this big lead you boys have cooked up?" McCarter asked impatiently after they had been riding for several minutes without so much as a peep from Dupont. "Did somebody finally claim the credit for the blast at the Louvre?"

Dupont frowned at the sound of McCarter's British accent. "I was given to understand you were all Americans."

"Can't trust anybody these days, mate," McCarter noted. "Let's hope the rest of the information you boys have is a little more reliable."

"All you need to know, Monsieur Dupont," Katz calmly explained, "is that for the hopefully brief time we will be spending together, you are our employee. Our nationalities have no bearing on the success or failure of this mission. The level at which you cooperate with us, however, could have a substantial impact on what my friends and I can accomplish while here in France. *Comprenez-vous?*"

"Oui. Je comprends." Dupont gritted the words from his mouth as though he were straining nails through his teeth. "I understand."

Katz smiled. "Good. Now back to the lead that UCLAT was working on. What have you come up with?"

Dupont sighed. "We think we may have discovered the identity of the terrorist responsible for the massacre."

"Don't tell us the bastard was stupid enough to be carrying a wallet?" Gary Manning guessed.

"No," Dupont answered. "Even if he had run onto the stage at the Louvre with a copy of his birth certificate in his pocket, it wouldn't have helped us. No one on the stage when the bomb went off survived the explosion, and many were essentially reduced to a pile of nothing."

"Which means that, in some cases, identification through dental records is next to impossible," Calvin James concluded.

"Precisely," Dupont said. "Our search teams have located pieces of bone and flesh as far as two hundred and fifty feet away from the site of the assault. Individual teeth have been recovered, but so far nothing substantial enough to enable dental records to be used for identification. We'll probably have to depend upon inquiries from victims' families before we know for sure the names of everyone killed."

"If there was nothing left of the terrorist but a puff of smoke and memories," Encizo began, "then how did UCLAT nail down his ID?"

"Shortly after the blast," Dupont responded, "police found a Volkswagen bus that had been abandoned near the Pont du Carrousel. That is a bridge just across one of the Louvre's main entrances. The keys to the VW were still in the ignition."

"An open invitation to steal the bus," Katz guessed. "But the police got there first."

"Only just." Dupont swerved the BMW around a slower moving Simca. "By then they were on the lookout for anyone behaving suspiciously. They observed two individuals approach the Volkswagen and apprehended the pair just before they drove away. Neither of the men was licensed to drive."

McCarter glanced out his window and subdued the urge to light up a Player's cigarette. Dupont was dragging out the details of UCLAT's investigation as though he were getting paid by the minute. "And running the Volkswagen through registration gave you the name of a probable suspect with a penchant for blowing himself up in front of millions of viewers on the telly."

"The VW was registered to a Jean-Paul Albert," Dupont explained. "We checked out his address, but of course he was not there. Neighbors confirmed that he was the owner of the Volkswagen, but could tell us little else. Albert was not much of a socializer. He kept pretty much to himself."

"How did this Albert character manage to pass through security?" Manning asked, aware as he did so that their BMW had left the road out of Orly and was now speeding along the *autoroute* into Paris. "Assuming there was a security check made on those attending the ceremony."

"There was," Dupont confirmed. "Albert was able to slip through by posing as a reporter for the newspaper *Le Figaro*. His press card was authentic and the name shown on the card also appeared on the master list of individuals scheduled to attend the broadcast, but the newspaper has since confirmed it has no one named Jean-Paul Albert on its staff. We did run a cross-reference computer search on the name to determine if it had been used before in such a ploy. Coincidentally or not, the name belonged to a man from Monpazier, a town in the south of France."

"Were you able to question him?" Calvin James asked the next logical question.

"No, unfortunately." Dupont reported. "The man from Monpazier was killed in a battle with the Germans during the First World War."

Still upset that he had been reduced by his superiors to little more than a glorified chauffeur, Dupont mentally reviewed his impressions of the men he had met at Orly. The five were a group of contradictions. They had flown to Paris aboard a United States Air Force jet, and yet only one or two of the men had American accents.

If they were not all Americans, why was UCLAT pulling out all stops to assist them? Who in the U.S. had that kind of pull? Traditionally UCLAT shunned external interference. Dupont supposed the five could be associated with the CIA, but something he could not quite put his finger on convinced him otherwise.

"After you register at your hotel and have had a chance to get organized I will take you to see Henri Ferronier," the French antiterrorist offered.

"How's he figure into the picture?" Rafael Encizo quizzed.

"Monsieur Ferronier is the *Ministre d'État*," answered Dupont. "It is his responsibility to oversee the internal affairs of France. In that capacity, he was one of three public officials invited to participate in the Louvre celebration. Monsieur Ferronier broke his ankle earlier in the day and was unable to appear at the broadcast."

"Was the public informed about Ferronier's accident?" Katz wanted to know.

"There was no time," Dupont said. "An announcement was to have been made during the course of the program. Ferronier's broken ankle seems to have saved his life.''

"At least for now," McCarter countered, giving in to his desire for a cigarette as he rolled his window down a fraction of an inch to let out the smoke. "Forget the hotel—we'll catch that act later. Right now, I think we'd like to meet with Ferronier."

"I agree with Mr. Black," Katz added, referring to McCarter's cover name. "If the brains behind the Louvre massacre expected Ferronier to die when your bogus reporter from *Le Figaro* hit the stage, then it's reasonable to expect they'll be disappointed to learn he's survived the attack."

Dupont smiled smugly. "UCLAT is not without its merits, Mr. Gray. We reached the same conclusion immediately, which is why we've had Monsier Ferronier's residence under our protection shortly after this miserable business began."

"All the same," the Israeli insisted, "we would still like the opportunity to discuss the matter with Monsieur Ferronier."

"As you wish," Dupont said without enthusiasm.

Thirty minutes and innumerable turns later, Dupont pulled their BMW onto the rue Copernic. Ferronier lived at the Hôtel St. Étienne, one of the many mansion-sized homes favored by the very rich in France.

"How many men do you have guarding the place?" asked Calvin James as they made their approach.

"A team of six men have been on duty since last night," replied Dupont. "I assure you, Monsieur Ferronier is perfectly safe."

At precisely that moment the roof of the Hôtel St. Étienne exploded into flames.

5

Phoenix Force reacted to the explosion faster than an astonished Edmond Dupont believed possible. The UCLAT agent scarcely had time to bring the BMW to a stop before his five mysterious passengers burst from the car in a flurry of motion.

Dupont was still recovering from the shock of the explosion when David McCarter, a Browning Hi-Power clutched in his right hand, threw open Dupont's door. The Briton looked warily from side to side for any signs of attack, then signaled for Dupont to climb out.

"Open the trunk!" the British commando ordered. Before Dupont stepped from the car he pulled a release lever, and the BMW's trunk automatically opened.

Calvin James withdrew his .45-caliber Colt Commander from his shoulder rig and guarded the opposite side of the BMW as Manning, Katz and Encizo raced to the car's trunk for additional firepower.

One advantage of linking up with UCLAT was that this eliminated playing with customs officials in getting weapons into France. Phoenix Force had come to Paris expecting trouble, and the arsenal that accompanied them proved they were ready for it.

"Mr. Black!" Manning called to McCarter as he removed the Briton's Mac-10 from the trunk and passed it over.

"Cheers," McCarter said as he strapped the Ingram over his shoulder and stuffed two spare magazines into the pockets of his coat.

A second explosion ripped apart more of the impressive Ferronier estate as Encizo's hands closed around his Heckler and Koch MP-5 machine gun. A silencer was attached to the H&K's barrel.

For backup Encizo had a Walther PPK tucked away in the holster he wore under his left arm. His Mark I Gerber fighting dagger was clipped at the small of his back.

Yakov Katzenelenbogen scooped his Uzi 9 mm SMG into his left hand. "That cuts it, Manning. Let's go!"

Gary Manning slammed the trunk shut. Like the rest of his teammates, the big Canadian had his preferences when it came to personal side arms. At the moment top honors went to the durable and deadly Eagle .357 Magnum.

A product of Israeli Military Industries, the Eagle first came to Manning's attention during Phoenix Force's unauthorized mission into Israel. Since that time the IMI powerhouse had helped keep Manning among the living more times than the Canadian cared to remember. What he did know was that when he needed it most, the Eagle never let him down.

As Manning ran from the rear of the BMW he saw that Edmond Dupont had armed himself with a 9 mm MAB-designed Model F-1 pistol. The French semiautomatic had a detachable box magazine containing fifteen rounds.

Manning hoped the arrogant Dupont knew how to use it.

Dupont had stopped the BMW across from the stone portico leading into the Hôtel St. Étienne. Two other vehicles, a Peugeot sedan and a Mercedes 500 SEL, were parked on their side of the street. Both cars appeared empty, but James wanted to make sure. Anyone ruthless enough to engineer the bombing at the Louvre would not hesitate to shoot an opponent in the back.

Cautiously James advanced the short distance up the street to examine the interiors of both automobiles. The Peugeot was empty. The Mercedes was not. Sprawled atop each other in the front seat were the bodies of two male Caucasians. Dark red blood and gray brain matter were splattered across the car's dashboard and stained the luxurious seats.

James frowned and rejoined the others as they moved across the boulevard in the direction of Ferronier's home.

"Got a couple of sleepers," James reported when Manning asked.

"Which car?" Dupont demanded.

"The Mercedes," replied James. "Head shots for the pair of them. Are they yours?"

"Yes," Dupont said, "UCLAT."

The flames crackling over the roof of the mansion lit up the dark winter sky with alternating flashes of red and orange. The smell of burning wood filled the air. The sound of a single gunshot reached their ears.

"How many entrances are there?" Katz demanded.

"Just two," Dupont answered. "One through the portico and the other exits onto a small street in back. We had men stationed at both."

Encizo motioned to Manning. "Mr. Green and I will swing around to the rear of the place," the Cuban offered, using the Canadian's cover name. "See you on the inside."

"Count on it," Katz promised as Encizo and Manning hurried up the street. The Israeli turned to Dupont. "Do you want to stay out here?"

The UCLAT man shook his head. "I cannot. They murdered my friends."

"Very well," Katz said as he signaled to McCarter and James. "Gentlemen?"

Gray smoke pushed through the curved brick entrance to the Ferronier property as Calvin James led the group forward. They were halfway across the street, when three gun-wielding figures suddenly emerged from the portico.

"Comment?" the lead gunman gasped in surprise at the unexpected sight of James. *"Tue-les!"* he screamed to his partners, raising his Llama Omni for what he thought would be an easy kill.

The loser's right index finger curled around the Llama's trigger just as James's Colt beat the killer to the punch. Twice the black Phoenix warrior's .45 snarled out its terrible message of doom. The close-range slugs ended the target's life in less than the blink of an eye.

One bullet drilled a gusher through the Frenchman's throat. Blood flowed from the wound like a leaking dike as bits of thyroid gland washed to the pavement. The Colt's second shot was just as deadly, driving through the dying man's chest directly over the right lung. Air hissed from the organ as the killer and his Llama Omni both crashed to the ground.

Katz and McCarter were equally fast to react. James's would-be assassin was still playing catch the bullets when the Israeli and Englishman each opened fire scant heartbeats before their opponents did.

Katz's foe was a shaggy-haired brute with dull-looking eyes and a brain to match. The terrorist was puzzled. Nobody ever said a word to him about getting caught, so what the hell was going on? The one-armed warrior had to be blind not to see the French MAS assault rifle that was aimed directly at him.

But something was terribly wrong. Although the French gunman blasted away with a 3-round burst of fire, not one of his shots knocked the old man down. The terrorist knew he had never been much of a sharpshooter, but the man he was trying to kill was less than thirty feet away. How could he have missed?

The answer became clear as a molten sensation of pain spread from sternum to groin down the gunman's torso. The truth registered just as he slipped into the cold arms of death. Of course, he thought. The old man had shot him. That explained why his aim was...

The second terrorist had even less luck than his friend. He managed to launch only a single .45 ACP rocket from his Astra A-80 before McCarter's Browning Hi-Power brought the killer's quest for victory down to earth. The dumbstruck killer accepted his fate without much of a fight—a wise decision considering the effect a couple of 9 mm bullets from McCarter's Browning had on his chances for survival.

The brokenhearted terrorist dropped his A-80, clasping his hands over the gaping hole in his chest. His legs folded beneath him, and he toppled to the ground.

Edmond Dupont's eyes blinked in disbelief. *Bon Dieu de merde!* He had never seen anything like this in his life. The three killers charging at them had been disposed of in less time than it took to down a beer.

Who were these ferocious fighters from America? They had reacted to the attack with an automatic response that was nothing short of fantastic. Dupont felt like an incompetent fool, the equivalent of a rookie agent fresh out of school.

Three killers had attacked them and he had not so much as fired a single bullet. Uncontrollably Dupont's face flushed with a combination of anger and shame.

"Time to move," James said.

"Right," McCarter added grimly, stepping over the trio of bodies as flames consumed more of the root of the Ferronier estate. "Things are getting hot."

GARY MANNING and Rafael Encizo were in the yard of the residence next to Ferronier's when the gunfight broke out on the rue Copernic. They listened to determine if they should return to aid their friends, but concluded that doubling back was unnecessary after the shooting abruptly ceased. No matter who had initiated the disturbance, the Cuban and the Canadian knew enough of their partners combined combat skills to believe that Phoenix Force had come out on top.

Confident that Katz and the others were all right, Manning and Encizo hurried alongside a high brick wall until they reached the bars of an iron gate. Encizo gave the barrier a nudge with his hand. It was locked.

"No problem," Manning said. "Stand back."

One shot from Manning's .357 Eagle had the locked gate swinging open on its hinges.

"So much for the lock," Encizo commented.

"That's what I call my keynote address," the Canadian returned.

Manning and Encizo emerged from the gate and onto the street behind the Ferronier property. Unlike the rue Copernic this smaller thoroughfare was more like an alley. The few cars parked on the road were arranged in a row on the far side of the street.

Light coming from the fire of the burning Hôtel St. Étienne bathed the narrow roadway in flickering yellow patterns. There was a Saab 900 Turbo parked directly across from the gate. With Encizo covering him, Manning ran to check out the car.

Slumped together in the front seat were two dead men—more of Dupont's UCLAT watchdogs, Manning guessed. Dupont had said that a team of six men had been assigned to guard Ferronier, which probably meant that another pair of bodies would eventually turn up.

"More UCLAT?" the Cuban asked Manning upon his return.

"Two. Just like the couple James found."

A sudden exchange of automatic weapons sounded from within the Ferronier estate as the two Phoenix Force members moved several feet to the left of the

open gate. This brought them to the Hôtel St.
Étienne's rear entrance. A door blocked the entry, but
a slight pull on its handle opened it easily.

Facing the Stony Man daredevils was a dimly lit
staircase rising sharply to the building's second floor.
A ceiling lamp at the top of the landing was partially
obscured by smoke. The noise of gunfire filtered down
the stairwell.

"Perfect place for a trap," stated Encizo.

"Getting caught in the middle could be murder."

The Cuban nodded in agreement. "Why don't you
run upstairs while I cover the landing."

"Why me?"

Encizo grinned. "'Cause McCarter's not available."

Manning rolled his eyes. "Lousy logic. But next
time it's your turn."

"You got a deal."

His Eagle .357 Magnum held in combat readiness,
and Encizo backing him up, Gary Manning began
climbing the stairs.

THE HÔTEL ST. ÉTIENNE WAS built around an open
courtyard that was large enough to double as a parking lot. Three vehicles occupied the space—a Rolls
Royce Silver Shadow, a Volvo and a sporty TR6 con-
vertible. A black Jaguar XJ6 was parked in the center
of a trio of single garages that faced onto the
courtyard.

These were the first things Calvin James noticed as
he stepped through the smoke-filled portico and onto
the Hôtel St. Étienne property. Yakov Katzenelenbogen and David McCarter quickly followed, with Edmond Dupont bringing up the rear.

"We've got to hurry," James said, his voice full of urgency. The flames eating away at the roof of the building were already consuming portions of the structure's second floor, and the temperature inside the courtyard was increasing at an alarming rate. "The way the fire's going, if Ferronier isn't already dead, he'll check out as a baked potato."

"Or at the very least a French fry," McCarter noted dryly.

"Monsieur Ferronier's primary living quarters and his study are upstairs and to the left," Dupont informed the men.

"Mr. Black and I will check it out," Katz told the man from UCLAT. "You and Mr. Blue," he added, referring to James, "will remain down here."

"We'll be waiting," Dupont responded.

Directly across the courtyard from the portico was an arched gateway. Katz and McCarter headed toward the staircase they could see beyond this entrance. They had reached the Silver Shadow, when a SMG-toting killer suddenly appeared on the balcony overlooking the courtyard.

The two Phoenix Force pros caught sight of their enemy at roughly the same time, and both collapsed to the pavement as the killer opened fire from above. Hot bullets chopped across the body of the Rolls Royce in a thudding sweep from left to right. The Silver Shadow's windshield shattered with a crash, sprinkling broken glass everywhere.

The snarling assassin continued to fire, hosing the courtyard beneath him with lead. As long as he had ammunition for his MAT-49 the killer felt invincible. He abruptly learned the difference between fact and fiction midway through his French subgun's magazine.

Calvin James and Edmond Dupont had taken cover at the first hint of the assault from the balcony. When it became obvious to the former Navy SEALS man that Katz and McCarter had been singled out as the subgunner's only targets, James rose above the protection of the Triumph and unleashed the full power of his Colt Commander. A determined Dupont simultaneously began firing his Model F-1.

Slugs struck the startled killer from two sides as the myth of his invincibility evaporated in a crossfire of destruction. The killer lived long enough to realize that he was about to die, and then perished in a hellstorm of pain. A .45-caliber zinger fired by James tickled the subgunner's ribs before churning the thug's esophagus into a mass of stringy paste. The Phoenix commando's next shot bulldozed an unwanted avenue through the killer's stomach and up into his left lung, before it finally lodged itself in the muscles of his back.

The subgunner's MAT-49 was already slipping from the grip of dying fingers, when Dupont's Model F-1 pistol made the killer's death official. Two of Dupont's shots went high before the third 9 mm parabellum connected with the bridge of the assassin's nose, plowing through the frontal sinus cavity and cracking the skull apart as though it were an eggshell caught beneath the foot of an elephant.

Dead on his feet, the gunman heaved the MAT-49 into the air before toppling forward and chasing the subgun from the balcony to the hard reality of the courtyard below. The body hit the ground headfirst with a sickening crack of snapping vertebrae.

Katz and McCarter were on their feet at once, racing through the stone gateway and up the stairs before someone else could pin them down. The top of the steps opened onto a landing from which corridors ran to the left and right. The Phoenix duo headed left toward Ferronier's living quarters.

A thick layer of black lung-choking smoke greeted Katz and McCarter as they rushed along the hallway. The British commando kicked something and glanced down to see the body of a dead woman. She wore a maid's uniform and an expression of shock. Small wonder. The ribbon of red running under her chin meant that her throat had been slashed.

Farther down the corridor another victim was found, this one wearing a butler's uniform. Most of the dead man's face had been erased by a gunshot. Blood, brains and bits of bone decorated the grisly wound.

The corridor veered again to the left. Katz checked to make sure all was clear, and then he and McCarter rushed around the corner. Three doorways were on their immediate right, while a fourth waited to greet them at the end of the hallway.

A tremendous shudder shook the building as another part of the blazing roof caved in. Katz and McCarter made it to the first of the doorways and shoved it open. Inside was a bedroom whose furniture probably predated many modern nations. A swift examination of the room revealed it was deserted.

The same was true of the next room, which turned out to be an oversized linen closet. Gunfire sounded from somewhere else on the floor as they continued their search. The third doorway opened onto a small bedroom that was also empty.

Fearing the worst, the Israeli and the Briton advanced toward the final door. McCarter twisted the doorknob and opened the door onto what was obviously Ferronier's private office. The walls of the room were lined with books from the floor to the ceiling. An oak desk dominated the far corner of the room, and sitting behind it, gagged and bound to his chair, was the *Ministre d'État*, Monsieur Ferronier.

Katzenelenbogen and McCarter ran forward into the room. The Israeli loosened the Frenchman's bonds, while McCarter placed his fingers to Ferronier's neck to check for a pulse. Although he had been beaten severely about the face, the *Ministre d'État* was alive.

"The bastards were going to cook him alive!" McCarter declared.

"Which is what's going to happen to us if we don't get the hell out of here!" Katz shouted.

Another tremor tore through the building just as the last of the ropes binding Ferronier came free. McCarter removed the gag covering the older man's mouth, then pushed Ferronier's chair back from the desk. Maintaining his grip on the Browning Hi-Power with his right hand, and doing his best to avoid banging the cast on Ferronier's broken ankle, the able-bodied Briton bent and hefted the minister's unconscious form over his left shoulder.

The temperature inside the room had skyrocketed and the thick, heavy black smoke made it impossible to clearly see the books lining the walls of Ferronier's office. Sweat glistened on the men's foreheads and the superheated air clawed at their lungs with each labored breath they took. It would soon be impossible to breathe.

"Have you got him?" Katz questioned.

"I've got him," replied McCarter, wiping the back of his hand that held the Hi-Power across his brow.

"I'll lead and you follow," Katz hollered over the roar of the flames that were devouring the building. "And don't get lost!"

Not bloody likely, thought McCarter.

6

Stefan and Phillipe Chompré ran along the upstairs hallway of the Ferronier estate. Full-time hoodlums and part-time firebugs, the Chompré brothers had jumped at the opportunity to get paid for a torch job.

Neither of the brothers had ever lasted on a legitimate job longer than a couple of weeks. Even their mother, recognizing them for the useless trash they were, had kicked them out of the house and onto the street while they were still in their teens.

A month later, Madame Chompé perished in a fiery blaze. There was no question that the fire that killed the woman and reduced her home to a smoldering ash heap had been deliberately set, but the police were unable to prosecute those responsible for the crime.

Madame Chompré's two sons were prime suspects in the case. The confrontation with their mother and their subsequent banishment from the Chompré household had been common knowledge among the people of their neighborhood. But because concrete evidence against them was virtually nonexistent, neither was charged with their mother's murder.

Setting fire to their family home was the brothers' first taste of pyromania. In the years that followed, the Chomprés torched more than a dozen other buildings, all of them owned by people who had somehow angered the two volatile men.

The deal to torch the Ferronier mansion was straightforward: they were simply to burn the *Ministre d'État*'s home to the ground.

They had been informed that something rather unpleasant had been planned for Ferronier and members of his staff, but the two Chompré hoodlums were only to worry about the matchworks part of the operation. Carrying out their end of the deal would add thousands of francs to their pockets.

There was no reason for the brothers not to accept the generous offer. If something bad was going to happen to the *Ministre d'État* and his staff, it would come to pass with or without their involvement. If they were not paid to torch the Ferronier estate, the money would go to someone else. And that would never do.

Only something had gone wrong. Alerted by gunfire from the rue Copernic, the Chompré brothers had interrupted their fun with flames in time to witness one of their comrades complete a death dive from the balcony overlooking the mansion's courtyard.

The two firebugs had no intention of sharing the dead man's fate. To hell with the job and to hell with collecting their fee.

They had entered the Hôtel St. Étienne through its back entrance, and it was toward this avenue of freedom that the two hoodlums fled. Their car was parked downstairs. All they had to do was get to their Citroën and they were home free.

Except for the fact that the two men ran head-on into Gary Manning as they charged down the stairs.

Stefan Chompré gasped at the sight of the wide-shouldered stranger blocking the stairway. He tried to brake his descent, but his brother, unable to stop, shoved him forward. The elder Chompré's hand flashed to his belt and came back holding a knife with a seven-inch blade.

The Eagle .357 in Manning's fist screamed twice, and the powerful Magnum filled the narrow staircase with the clamor of portable thunder. Both shots from the Eagle struck the Canadian's attacker at point blank range.

Stefan Chompré shrieked as a double dose of agony made instant hell out of his universe. The French pyro felt a burning sensation tear straight through his chest, while another volcano of pain ripped into his stomach. Blood spit from his mouth, and his knife was forgotten. Chompré's knees buckled under his weight as he died and toppled down the stairs.

Manning had half a second to brace himself before the dead weight of the falling man slammed into him. Staying upright and on his feet was impossible. The best Manning could manage was to grab hold of the dead man's body for support and enjoy the bumpy ride to the bottom of the steps.

Rafael Encizo moved out of the way as Manning and the dead man came bouncing down the stairs. Momentarily distracted, the Cuban regained control of the situation just as Phillipe Chompré whipped out a RG 31 .38 Special. The panicking younger brother got off a single shot that popped into the doorframe next to where Encizo was standing. Encizo's Heckler and Koch MP-5 then got into the act and the last of the Chompré brothers was no more.

Dropping the .38 Special as though it had suddenly become too hot to hold, Phillipe Chompé played unwanted host to six of the H&K's finest. The French firebug could never have concocted such a vicious world of hurt. His lungs, his genitals, his heart, the side of his neck, even his right kneecap—everything was blasted into orbit at once.

Phillipe Chompré gulped and tasted something warm and salty, then sank into a forward roll that sent him spinning down the steps after his brother. All the way down he could hear his mother laughing.

Encizo helped Manning pick himself up off the floor just as the body of the younger firebug rolled to a halt. Manning shook his head to clear his thoughts and was surprised to discover that the Eagle .357 was still locked in his fist.

"You okay?" asked Encizo.

"Sure," returned Manning. "Like your typical ten pounds of shit in a five-pound bag. No broken bones, though, so I guess I'll live."

"Good" the Cuban said as he jumped over the bodies of the Chompré brothers and then started running up the stairs. "Come on, I'll race you to the top!"

Manning shrugged off the hurt from his fall and hurried up the steps. Encizo beat him to the landing, but only by a couple of seconds. Smoke filled the corridors and heat from the fire on the roof bordered on the unbearable. A shudder rumbled through the inferno, prompting both Phoenix Force veterans to wish they were somewhere else.

With Encizo in the lead they followed a hallway that took them closer to where a portion of the fire-weakened roof had already collapsed. Flames had charred the wallpaper to sheets of crispy black, and yards of carpeting had ignited and burned. The soles of their shoes felt as if they were melting.

As Encizo and Manning rounded a bend in the corridor they tensed. Squinting through the haze and the smoke, they could make out shapes moving their way. Both men gripped their weapons tighter. The only way out of the fiery coffin lay ahead. If that meant battling more of those responsible for setting the blaze, it would have to be quick. In another minute anyone left on the second floor would be trapped in the fire.

Sweat stung Manning's eyes as he recognized the shapes emerging through the blinding smoke. Katz and McCarter! The British commando had an unconscious man draped over his shoulder and was allowing Katz to guide him through the smoke to safety.

A fresh tremor wracked the Hôtel St. Étienne to its foundations as Manning turned to Encizo and shouted, "There's our ticket!"

Forging onward, Manning and Encizo quickly joined forces with Katz and McCarter. Manning had no idea how far his British friend had carried his burden, but he could tell that the grueling combination of physical exertion and smoke inhalation had taken its toll. McCarter looked ready to drop.

Stepping to the Briton's side, the brawny Canadian lifted the inert form of the man he guessed to be the French *Ministre d'État* from McCarter's shoulder and onto his own. McCarter nodded in gratitude as Katzenelenbogen led them all through the maze of smoke now choking the second floor of the estate. They found the stairway leading to the courtyard and started down. Totally blinded when they finally reached the bottom, they were met by Calvin James and Edmond Dupont, who pulled them farther into the courtyard and away from the burning building.

James helped Manning ease Ferronier gently to the ground.

"Is he alive?" Dupont questioned.

James felt for a pulse. "Strong heartbeat, even though he looks like hell. Anybody else up there left to save?" he asked, turning to a weary McCarter.

"Not anymore," the Englishman replied. "We tumbled onto a couple of the hired help—a maid and a butler, I think—but they were already dead."

"And we discovered two more bodies out back of the place," said Manning. "Probably part of the UCLAT team you had on guard here, Dupont."

"Merde!" was the UCLAT agent's initial response. "That makes four of the six that we know about for sure."

"At least we were able to save Monsieur Ferronier," Katz stated. "The killers had him tied to a chair in his office. He would have died if we hadn't found him."

"What about the killers?" asked Dupont.

"As far as I know, all dead," Katz told him.

"And that includes the two we ran into," Encizo added.

The whole second floor of the Hôtel St. Étienne was devoured by the flames of the fire. A tremendous whoosh of air washed over them as more of the roof caved in. The shattering crash almost masked a noise that none of them was expecting to hear.

"Shit!" James swore in protest as the black Jaguar suddenly came to life, shooting from the center garage onto the courtyard and screeching in a sharp turn to the left. James caught a fleeting glimpse of two male figures riding in the front seat. Then the sports car flew through the portico entrance and was gone.

James ran after the Jag. "Come on, Dupont! We're going for a ride!"

7

"The keys, man! Give me the keys!" James shouted
to Dupont.

The two men sprinted through the Hôtel St.
Étienne's arched portico and across the rue Copernic
to where Dupont's BMW was parked. James held his
arm behind him relay-style, then really pounded his
feet on the street once the keys were placed in his hand.

The black Phoenix Force commando was sitting at
the wheel of the BMW with the motor running when
Dupont finally climbed in on the passenger's side.
They were off and away as soon as James heard Dupont's door close.

The BMW was facing east. The Jaguar carrying the
leftovers of the Henri Ferronier hit team had headed
west. James took a deep breath and checked for oncoming traffic; they would go west, too.

Screeching away from the side of the road, James
threw the BMW into a sharp U-turn, throwing Dupont against his door. The BMW's radials clung to the
pavement like a surefooted cat. When the car came out
of its turn Dupont settled into place and grabbed for
his seat belt. James mashed the accelerator to the floor
and the BMW shot forward.

James had a good view of the rue Copernic. At the far end of the boulevard he could see the Jaguar they wanted to catch. Only two other cars separated them. The driver of the Jaguar was speeding, but he wasn't driving as fast as he would go if he knew someone was following him.

James waited for an oncoming car to pass, then whipped the BMW into the opposing lane. Headlights from another car were quickly approaching as he gunned the engine, sending Dupont's pride and joy alongside and then in front of a slower moving vehicle.

"Hold tight," James cautioned his passenger before pulling out into the opposing lane of traffic again—this time to pass a car crammed with teenagers. Up ahead the formidable-looking delivery truck was driving straight for them.

"We're not going to make it," Dupond screamed.

"Sure we are," James assured him.

The kid at the wheel of the compact glanced to his left at the passing BMW. He yelled something neither James nor Dupont could hear, and the VW suddenly gained speed.

"The little shit's racing with us," the Phoenix Force pro growled.

"And helping us smash into the truck."

James saw quickly that Dupont was right. If the kid did not slow down there would be a pileup for sure.

"Show the punk your gun!" James ordered.

Dupont did, but the only response he got was more giggles from the teenage hotrod.

James's eyes widened. Another fifteen seconds and the furniture truck would be on them. He felt cool night air blow into the car as Dupont lowered his window. Then the UCLAT agent stuck his Model F-1 semiauto pistol outside and fired a single warning shot into the sky. That did the trick.

Reacting to Dupont's 9 mm. parabellum message, the kid wheeling the car sobered up on the spot and hit the brakes. The compact dropped out of the BMW's way and came to a skidding stop that caught the driver of another vehicle unprepared. The two cars connected with a resounding crunch.

James cut the wheel hard to the right, pulling the BMW into line just as the furniture truck rushed past them like a dinosaur on wheels. Dupont sighed with relief.

"What's all the noise?" James asked. "I told you we'd make it. Piece of cake."

"I prefer croissants," Dupont returned.

They reached a busy intersection and James scanned the rows of cars as he eased the BMW into the flow of traffic. The Jaguar they were chasing had vanished.

"Damn!" James swore. "We lost them."

"No!" Dupont pointed to his left where the errant XJ6 was negotiating a complete revolution of the traffic circle.

"Yeah, there they are," James acknowledged, perturbed at how slow the cars in the roundabout moved. "But we'll never catch them at this rate. How do we get the cars ahead of us to drive faster?"

"This is France. I'm afraid that's impossible."

Halfway around the intersection James watched helplessly as Henri Ferronier's stolen Jaguar broke away from the pack and sped out of sight. The Phoenix Force warrior drummed his fingers across the steering wheel and continued around the traffic circle. At least the hoods in the Jag were oblivious to the fact that they were being tailed, and therefore had not resorted to evasive maneuvers.

After what seemed to James like an eternity, the traffic finally circumnavigated the roundabout. The Phoenix Force commando found the opening he wanted and immediately fed the BMW's engine all the fuel it could use. The avenue was extremely wide and provided ample room for James to put the BMW through its paces.

"What do you think?" James searched through the windshield for signs of the missing Jaguar.

"My guess is they have stayed on this street," Dupont replied. "It's not as if they know we are behind them."

"That's what I was thinking."

"Perhaps you would like me to drive?"

"No, thanks. I'm doing fine."

"Is that what they call it in America when you almost collide with a furniture truck?"

"No," James said excitedly, "that's what it means when my sharp eyes locate the Jaguar you let slip away."

"Where?"

"About three blocks ahead of us. I just saw them change lanes."

Dupont leaned to the edge of his seat and squinted. *"Oui,* it is them. What do you propose?"

"Let's try to get a little closer."

James maneuvered the BMW to the boulevard's inside lane and pushed the accelerator to the floor. The car leapt forward, eliminating the distance between the two vehicles with each passing second. He waited until they were almost parallel to the Jag, then slacked off speed, keeping the BMW's front bumper lined up with the Jaguar's left rear door.

James was confident he could use the BMW as a battering ram to force the Jaguar off the road, but such a desperate tactic was risky. The boulevard was lined with pedestrians on both sides, each person a potential victim should the Jaguar become a runaway.

Having Dupont try to shoot out one of the car's tires or even the car's driver could produce the same horrific results. Not only that, James reasoned, but if Dupont happened to miss, then their adversaries would have the chance to retaliate with some firepower of their own. As the Phoenix Force pro scoured his mind for a viable solution that would not endanger the general public, the matter was taken out of his hands. The hit man driving the Jaguar cut back on his speed, simultaneously rolling down his window.

"Shit," James protested as the business end of a Smith and Wesson Model 57 .41 Magnum was pointed in his direction.

James slammed his foot on the BMW's brakes, stopping Dupont's car just as the killer's Model 57 was fired. The shot fell short of its goal and screamed off the BMW's hood with a teeth-gnashing whine as the S&W's recoil caused the Jaguar's driver to fight for control of the car.

The sports car swerved awkwardly from side to side. Dupont muttered something to himself in French. Calvin James half expected the gunman to try for an encore, but the hood driving the Jaguar had learned his lesson. The second the killer regained command of his car, and the Jaguar accelerated up the boulevard in a blinding flash of speed.

"Well?" Dupont commented.

"I think you could safely say they spotted us," James said, giving the BMW enough gas to send them partway to the moon. "What do you say we go catch them?"

"A splendid idea."

Dupont opened the glove compartment and removed the handset for the BMW's two-way radio. While James closed the gap between themselves and the Jaguar, Dupont updated UCLAT headquarters on their present situation, ending his transmission with a brief rundown of what had transpired at the home of Ministre d'État Ferronier.

"Est-ce que toutes les investigations de UCLAT sont aussi amusantes?" Calvin James asked once Dupont was off the radio.

"No," Dupont returned, "all UCLAT investigations are not this much fun. And thank goodness for that! I see that Mr. Gray is not the only one of your party to speak French."

James smiled. "We all have hidden talents."

A quarter mile in front of their position the Jaguar narrowly avoided a head-on collision as it turned left off the boulevard. The BMW faced and avoided the same accident twenty seconds later.

One avenue dissolved into the next as the two vehicles played cat and mouse. James did not let the elusive Jaguar out of his sight. Dupont contributed to the chase by keeping a lookout for vehicles entering the boulevard from side streets.

They rounded a curve and flew through a colorfully lit intersection. An old man shook his angry fist at them as they passed. James caught a glimpse to his left of the ORTF, the French national radio-and-television building. Then they were crossing the Seine at the Pont de Grenelle.

The Left Bank traffic seemed in no particular hurry to get anywhere. Both James and the gunman driving the Jaguar had no choice but to slow down. Neither of the two cars lost or gained ground.

"Where's a big traffic jam when you need one?" Calvin James wondered aloud. "If we really slowed down I could probably hop out and catch the bastards on foot."

"You may get to," Dupont advised. "Look."

As they watched, a passenger bus pulled in front of the Jaguar, causing the sports car and everyone else to slow their speed even more. The Jaguar attempted to pass, but was forced to get back in line when a second bus traveling in the opposite direction almost ran the Jag over.

Five cars separated the two vehicles. The BMW's speedometer showed fifty kilometers, or roughly thirty miles per hour. Traffic coming at them in the opposite lane was bumper to bumper.

"We'll take them once the bus we're following stops to pick up riders," James said. "That should box the Jag in long enough for us to make our move."

"On foot?" Dupont wanted to make certain he understood correctly.

"Oui," James supplied, patting his hand over the reassuring feel of his Colt Commander. "On foot."

The brake lights on the bus glowed brighter. All traffic on their side of the street started to slow. Dupont leaned out and confirmed that they were coming to a bus stop.

"Great," the Phoenix pro said, reacting to the news. "Get ready. I hope you don't mind leaving your car in the middle of the road."

"What are they going to do? Give me a ticket?"

The bus finally came to a stop. James swallowed as his eyes swept across to Dupont. The UCLAT agent was poised on the edge of his seat, his 9 mm Model F-1 pistol gripped firmly in his hand.

"Time to run." Calvin James threw open his door and was about to step outside, when the Jaguar leapt forward and unexpectedly jumped the curb on its right.

Frightened pedestrians scattered as the black sports car drove down the sidewalk. James slammed his door closed and then as fast as he dared, followed the Jag's example. The BMW was a hundred feet from the XJ6 and closing.

"What the hell?" James swore.

The Jaguar turned into the row of buildings fronting the street and disappeared. When Calvin James came to the spot where the Jag had vanished, the mystery was solved. A short driveway led to a tunnel set into the wall, over which hung a flashing blue neon sign advertising *Parking*.

The Phoenix Force commando sent the BMW speeding into the underground parking lot, twisting the steering wheel with a steady right-hand turn as the entrance to the lot corkscrewed them after the Jaguar. The BMW's tires sang against the pavement. Somewhere below, the Jag's tires were doing the same.

They came out of the corkscrew and onto a straightaway. The Jaguar was less than a hundred feet ahead. James pushed the acclerator to the floor as the XJ6 rocked to a halt, its doors flying open. Two men ran from the car. The driver turned toward the rapidly advancing BMW long enough to unload another shot from his S&W Model 57. The hastily aimed .41 Magnum slug missed. The pair from the Jaguar continued running, shoving their way through swinging doors at the far end of the lot.

Calvin James brought the BMW to a quick stop behind the Jaguar. He and Dupont leapt from the car. James's Combat Colt was drawn and ready. Dupont was equally prepared to use his MAB Model F-1.

"Cover me," James shouted. "I'll see if they're expecting us."

With Dupont following close on his heels, the Phoenix hardshot rammed his shoulder into the swinging doors and pushed his way through, dropping to the floor and into a forward body roll as a bullet slapped wood on the doorframe over head. Dupont's F-1 answered in response from between the swinging doors.

James rose to a kneeling stance, but no more shots were fired. Dupont darted into what was evidently a stairwell. Screams suddenly filled the air. James and Dupont began to climb the short flight of stairs, each man training his handgun on a different section of stairway.

The screams continued, and they heard footsteps charging in their direction. James and Dupont aimed their weapons at the top of the staircase, but held their fire when a couple of terrified teenagers came running down the stairs. The sight of two armed men did not calm the frightened kids. The young boy and girl jumped to the bottom of the steps and ran through the swinging doors and out of harm's way.

Calvin James reached the top of the stairs first, although Dupont was hot on his trail. Mild surprise registered on the black Phoenix Force commando's face. The chase across Paris from the Hôtel St. Étienne had led them to an underground bowling alley.

More than a dozen alleys were stretched out to the left, as were a line of racks containing bowling balls. Straight ahead was a carpeted aisle running the width of the building. An arcade of coin-operated video games and pinball machines occupied much of the area to the right. The cashier's stand and shoe-rental counter were stationed midway down the aisle.

Weekend bowlers at the alley had reacted to the exchange of gunfire in one of two ways. Most had panicked as the teenage couple had done and scattered for the nearest exits; the others had remained frozen in fear, huddled together in trembling groups or lying flat on the floor with their hands over their heads. A chorus of frightened whimpers permeated the building.

James felt certain that the thugs from the Jaguar were still in the bowling alley—the tension level in the room would not be as high if the killers had escaped. James and the UCLAT agent advanced quietly, both men keeping low, allowing the racks of bowling balls to serve as a barrier between themselves and the alleys to their left.

James stopped and listened, his ears straining to pick out anything that might indicate their enemy's whereabouts. It was useless. Between the electronic music playing on the various video games and a telephone that rang incessantly from somewhere behind the shoe-rental counter, the killers could have made all the noise they wanted to without risking detection.

Five feet in front of James was a break in the racks of bowling balls and a set of steps that led down off the aisle to the alleys. Crossing the space would make catching a bullet a cinch if the killers were expecting him. The Phoenix Force pro decided to see.

Taking a bowling ball from the lowest level of the rack, James placed the sixteen-pound ball on the carpet and pushed. Silently the ball rolled along the aisle and across the space separating the racks.

Crack! A .4l Magnum slug smashed into the bowling ball, blasting it apart as though it were made of rubber. Pieces of the bowling ball spread across the carpeted aisle. A female cringing beside a video game screamed.

One of the killers popped up from behind the shoe-rental counter where he had been hiding. The French hood was sporting a Star Model 28D/A 9 mm pistol. Presented with two possible targets, the confused creep glanced from Calvin James to Edmond Dupont, unsure of who to shoot first. The fraction of a heartbeat's hesitation cost him his life.

Like twin thunderclaps, James's Colt Commander and Dupont's F-l pistol lashed out at the indecisive thug. A pair of the Colt's .45-caliber manglers punched into the killer's chest. Ribs snapped like dry kindling. The sternum broke apart as though smashed by a hammer, and his right lung leaked air. Blood spurted from the wounds in a dark red fountain.

The shots from Dupont's weapon were equally effective in eliminating their enemy. One shot blipped the hit man through the center of his nose. The well-aimed 9 mm shot reduced cartilage and frontal bone to gritty bits of mush. The UCLAT agent's final bullet ripped into the doomed man's gut, gouging a hole through his liver before lodging itself in the spine.

The killer's Spanish army-issue Star Model 28D/A went flying and so did he, his lifeless hands waving in the air and his body tumbling dead to the floor with a sickening thump.

James raised his eyes over the rim of the bowling-ball racks in time to see the crud who had driven the Jag make a run for it down one of the alleys. The Phoenix Force commando rose to his feet and rushed the steps leading off of the aisle.

"Attendez!" James hollered for the hood to stop. As far as he knew the gunman was the sole survivor of the team assigned to hit the Hôtel St. Étienne. That made him especially important to Phoenix Force's mission in France; so far he was their only living link to the brains behind the bombing at the Louvre. *"Attendez!"*

The killer had no intention of surrendering to James. Ten feet from the end of the alley the gunman whirled on his feet and began hammering away with his Smith and Wesson Model 57, instinctivley homing in on the sound of James's voice.

Glass exploded as a pinball machine behind James was hit. A bowling ball next to the Phoenix Force commando's elbow shared the same fate. James dove for cover and came up fighting.

Now it's my turn, chump, he thought, letting his Colt Combat Commander do what it did best. The Phoenix pro's aim was true, each of his three shots striking flesh and bone and causing the killer to grunt with pain.

The S&W Model 57 sailed into the gutter. The killer turned, still on his feet. He tried to run, but he staggered and fell, sliding across the slick wooden floor and into the pins at the end of the alley. All of the pins went down with him.

So much for learning who engineered the attack on the Louvre. Disgusted, James reholstered his Colt.

"Are you all right, Monsieur Blue?" Dupont questioned.

"Just peachy," James answered. "I was sort of hoping we could take one of them alive."

"C'est la vie," Dupont said with a shrug.

Within a matter of minutes the bowling alley was swarming with police. Several patrons were treated for shock. An energetic gendarme questioned James and Dupont on specifics, but when Dupont presented his UCLAT ID and claimed silence in the interest of national security, neither he nor James were obliged to answer any of the policeman's questions.

While the gendarme turned his attention elsewhere, several of Dupont's UCLAT associates arrived with the rest of the Phoenix Force crew. As Dupont talked quietly with several of his fellow agents, James walked over to greet his friends.

"What kept you?" James asked.

Encizo pointed to the body sprawled at the end of the alley. "Looks like you started the game without us."

"No choice," James said. "There's another tough full of starch over where they rent the shoes. Dupont and I took him out together."

"What about the guy on the alley?" Katz quizzed.

James shook his head. "I tried to get him to throw in the towel, but he wouldn't listen to reason. He shot at me. I shot at him. He missed. I didn't."

"Really bowled him over with your charm," concluded McCarter. "Looks like you got all the pins down."

"With no time to spare," agreed James. "It was a real lucky strike."

"Not for him, it wasn't." Manning added. "He's as dead as they come."

"Yeah," James confirmed. "Sort of like a freeze-frame."

AN HOUR LATER, after he had been questioned by the police and sent home, one of the employees at the bowling alley placed a long-distance telephone call.

The caller phoned collect.

8

The weather report predicted a storm. Adolf Zeigler did not mind. Warm and secure in ODESSA's mountain *Hauptquartier* high in the Pyrenees, the Nazi general was not about to let a little extra snow and ice disrupt his plans. The news he had just received from Paris...well, that was another matter.

After such an auspicious beginning with the successful bombing at the Louvre, one would have thought the assassination of Ministre d'État Ferronier could have been handled with relative ease, especially when one considered that eight men had been sent to do the job.

Yet Henri Ferronier still lived!

The *Ministre's* home had been razed, many of his servants had been killed and the six-man government security contingent guarding Ferronier had been eliminated. So why in hell was old man Ferronier still alive? Obviously someone had intervened on the *Ministre d'État's* behalf. But who?

Zeigler intertwined his fingers and stretched, cracking his knuckles loudly with a satisfying crunch. Henri Ferronier was a fortunate man. Twice in one week Ferronier had escaped certain death. Did this mean the *Ministre* was destined to live? Of course not,

Zeigler concluded. It only meant that next time he would not send boys to do the work of men. Ministre d'État Ferronier represented a loose end that would have to be tied.

Zeigler scratched an itch at the back of his head. As sketchy as the information he received on the Ferronier situation was, one important aspect of the preliminary details disturbed him. Of the eight men contracted to kill Ferronier, the bodies of only six had been recovered.

What had happened to the remaining two men? Had they been captured? Zeigler's gendarme contact confirmed that this was not the case. Not that their being apprehended would have jeopardized the overall scheme of things. The men unaccounted for were common criminals, guns for hire with sawdust for brains. They could sing a duet for the police the whole night through and the authorities would learn nothing.

Even so, Zeigler would have felt better knowing what had become of the two killers. The one-eyed ODESSA general had learned years ago that left unattended, seemingly insignificant problems had a habit of escalating into major crises. He had that feeling about the pair of missing hit men.

"Herr Obergruppenführer?"

"Ja?" Zeigler turned from the picture window he was facing. "What is it, Schmidt?"

Rottenführer Schmidt held up the portable telephone he was carrying. "It is Dortmann, sir. He says it is urgent. Something about the incident in Paris."

"Very well." Zeigler held out his hand for the phone. "That will be all for now, Schmidt."

The ODESSA corporal dutifully clicked his heels. "I will be in the next room if you need me."

Zeigler waited for Schmidt to depart, then placed the receiver to his ear. *"Ja?"*

"Good evening," Dortmann said above the static on the line.

"Perhaps that description matches your evening," Zeigler countered. "Mine has been far from satisfactory. You have an urgent message for me, I am told."

"Yes, it concerns the results of tonight's activities in Paris," Dortmann said, deliberately avoiding specifics in case the line happened to be tapped.

"You are too late, I am afraid. I am already in possession of that information. The fish we sought has escaped our net. I've known for almost an hour now."

"Then you are privy to only half the story."

Zeigler absently ran his finger along the scar below his blind left eye. "Oh. And what is it you have to add?"

"Of the eight fishermen hired to deal with the fish, six went down with the ship. I am calling about the other two."

"What about them?"

"I just received word they were hooked far from the location of the original expedition."

"I see. And how are the two fishermen now?"

"They have joined their friends."

Zeigler grunted. All the men hired to dispose of Ministre d'État Ferronier could now be accounted for. Good.

"Tell me," ODESSA's second-in-command requested. "Do you know precisely how the fishermen were lost at sea?"

"Only regarding number seven and number eight. Their ship went down in a bowling alley on the Left Bank."

"Who sank it?"

"That's why I was contacted. Both fishermen were caught in a net thrown by two men—a French Caucasian and a black American."

Zeigler's throat tightened. "Go on."

"The Frenchman had connections where it counts. He had plenty of friends show up after the fishermen were gone. All the friends were with Industrie Français."

Or with some branch of the French secret service, Zeigler realized. "And the American?"

"He, too, was met by friends. Four of them. But my caller could not get near enough to determine nationalities."

Zeigler's internal warning system went haywire. His sightless eye began to twitch uncontrollably. "Describe the American's four companions."

"Three men who appeared to be in their thirties."

"And the fourth?" Zeigler's voice snarled out the question.

"An older man. Late fifties. Gray hair. A bit heavy and—"

"And he only had one arm!" Zeigler stated.

Dortmann sputtered over the static on the line. "He only had one arm, that is correct. But—"

"Never mind. You have done well. I will be in touch with you shortly."

Zeigler flipped the button to disconnect Dortmann's call, his fingers trembling with excitement and rage. So! Now it became clear why Ministre d'État

Ferronier had not been killed during the attack on his home. Now it became clear exactly who had intervened on Ferronier's behalf.

Ferronier's savior was none other than the one man Adolf Zeigler hated most in all the world: Colonel Yakov Katzenelenbogen! Zeigler's powerful hands curled into angry fists. He knew the Israeli colonel all too well.

Zeigler owed the loss of his eye and the gross disfiguration of his once-handsome features to the Jewish warrior. Katzenelenbogen had ripped Zeigler's face apart with a steel hook, then stabbed him in the chest with a bayonet, leaving him for the grave.

But Zeigler had not died. And he had learned to live with his blind left eye and the nervous smiles of the *Fräuleinen* when they got too close to his scarred face. Yes, the perennial Nazi recalled, he had much to thank his Israeli for. But he had even greater reasons for despising Katzenelenbogen. Some time ago ODESSA had aligned itself with a splinter group of the Baader-Meinhof terrorist gang in West Germany. The purpose of this union was to spearhead the seizure of a NASA missile site and to threaten to destroy major cities if demands were not met.

The plan nearly succeeded, would have succeeded, if Yakov Katzenelenbogen and his commando friends had not entered the fight. Instead the entire ODESSA-Baader-Meinhof operation had perished in dismal defeat.

So, now the Jewish *Scheiszer* was interfering in ODESSA's affairs once more. *Wunderbar*, Zeigler thought, chuckling softly to himself. Let the Jewish meddler stick his nose where it did not belong. History would not repeat itself. This time when the opposing forces clashed, things would be different. This time ODESSA would emerge victorious.

"Schmidt!" Zeigler called for his corporal.

In an instant the *Rottenführer* appeared.

"Ja, Herr Obergruppenführer?"

Zeigler returned the cordless telephone to Schmidt. "Tell Becker I want to see him at once."

Schmidt quickly departed to carry out Zeigler's orders.

As he waited for Johann Becker to arrive, Adolf Zeigler studied his reflection in the glass of the picture window that overlooked the Pyrenees. Zeigler was smiling. Never send a boy to do a man's job. The French boys had blown their chance of dealing with the Israeli colonel and his friends. Now it was a man's turn. Becker's turn.

Auf Wiedersehen, Katzenelenbogen. Your time has come.

9

Raymond Jouffreau was happy to work Sunday mornings because it meant he did not have to go to church. The Frenchman believed that religion had nothing to do with the concept of heaven and hell, and that a journey along the road to salvation did not begin with the daily observance of a strict set of rules.

Religion to Raymond Jouffreau meant kneeling, lots of kneeling. Good Catholics were not made; they were born. And it all started with the knees. Jouffreau was convinced that with knees of iron, any man could aspire to be Pope.

Raymond Jouffreau would never sit in the Vatican. No strength in the knees, he liked to tell his wife. His joints were like jelly. He was often seen walking with a limp—an affliction that struck at the oddest times, but most frequently when he had a free Sunday morning. This limp disappeared as soon as his wife left for church. The rate of his recovery was simply miraculous.

Raymond Jouffreau sat at his favorite table in the Café Alouette, drinking coffee and waiting for Napoléon to arrive. Napoléon—he did not know the Algerian's real name—was one of a handful of criminal informants who regularly made Jouffreau's job as a sergeant in the Gendarmerie Nationale that much easier.

Jouffreau was not wearing his uniform. He never did when he worked the streets. Broadcast the fact that you were a law enforcer and sources dried up faster than a prostitute's generosity when her customer's francs ran out. Jouffreau left his uniform hanging in his closet next to the suit he never wore to church.

The police sergeant looked across the the café's entrance as Napoléon entered. Napoléon was a swarthy fellow with small ears and squinty eyes who had the bad taste to always wear his shirt half unbuttoned, exposing the forest of hair sprouting from his chest. Napoléon insisted that this drove the many women in his life into states of sexual frenzy, but all it told Jouffreau was that some females had a fetish for mating with carpets.

"Bonjour," Napoléon greeted Jouffreau as he settled himself on the only other chair at Jouffreau's table. "What are we drinking?"

"I'm drinking coffee."

"Sounds good to me." Napoléon snapped his fingers at a passing waiter and ordered a cup for himself, then leaned across the table to confess, "Oh, what a time I had last night, let me tell you."

"I wish you wouldn't."

"'Louise' is what she calls herself. She's a beauty! She should have a flower named after her. *Mon Dieu*, what a garden of delights!"

"Spare me the details," Jouffreau said after the waiter delivered Napoléon's coffee. "It's too early in the day for me to listen to your fabricated exploits of the boudoir."

The Algerian looked hurt. "*Mon ami*, you do me a great injustice. Would someone as handsome as I have to dream up the kind of life that even Casanova would have envied? Of course not! Every word is true." He sipped his coffee. "Have you had breakfast?"

"No."

"Splendid! Neither have I." Napoléon pursed his lips. "You are buying, I presume?"

"I buy information, not rolls and butter." The police sergeant finished his coffee and pushed his chair away from the table. "See you next week, Napoléon. For old time's sake, I will pay for your coffee. *Au revoir.*"

The *pied-noir* shrugged indifferently. "Very well. Don't buy the best friend you have in Paris a small crumb to eat. I'm not hungry, anyway. I only thought breakfast was the least you could do for the man who could make you the hero of your department."

His curiosity piqued, Raymond Jouffreau remained seated. "All right. What have you got for me?"

"Not so fast. This will cost you a lot more than one measly meal."

"How much?"

"Ten thousand francs."

"Enjoy your coffee."

"You are too impatient, Jouffreau. The information I have to sell would be a bargain at twice the price, but I'm willing to let it go to you for a song because you are my friend."

Jouffreau pushed away from the table again. "You'll have to do better than that."

"Very well." The Algerian sighed. "The secret I sell concerns the horrible bombing at the Louvre."

Jouffreau nodded. "What about the bombing?"

Napoléon smiled. "I know who did it."

10

"The Ocs are a relatively loose band of individuals who want the south of France to become a completely autonomous state," Edmond Dupont informed the Phoenix Force warriors. "The nation created by this separation would be called 'Occitania'—hence the name chosen to represent members of the movement."

Dupont and the men of Phoenix Force were gathered in a soundproof conference room located at UCLAT's Paris headquarters.

"Have the Ocs been involved in terrorist activities?" Katz questioned.

Dupont's shoulders rose and fell. "Up to now, no. They have always sought to achieve their goal through political channels. Frankly, it never occurred to UCLAT that the Ocs might be behind the Louvre massacre."

"That's understandable," Gary Manning agreed. "My first guess would have been some of your Direct Action crazies. Since 1979 they have been responsible for a series of bank robberies and bombings of French government buildings."

"True. Among its other gripes," Dupont added, "Action Directe is vehemently opposed to what its members term 'American imperialism on French soil.'"

"Which would have made the celebration at the Louvre a likely target for the Direct Action bunch," Encizo said. "Since Direct Action linked up with the West German Red Army faction last year there has been a marked increase in terrorist activities throughout Europe."

Dupont made a sour face. "The partnership of Action Directe and the Red Army faction has been a headache for all of us. No sooner was their deplorable alliance announced than General René Audràn was executed in front of his home in a Paris suburb. General Audràn was in charge of the arms-sales program in the Defense Ministry. The poor man was butchered—gunned down by no less than eight .45-caliber bullets."

"And five days after that," Gary Manning recalled, "the same thing happened in Munich to one of West Germany's top weapons manufacturers."

"So neither Direct Action nor the Red Army faction would look forward to the United States increasing its military presence in France," stated McCarter. "But if these Ocs people are serious about seceding from France, then they wouldn't exactly welcome the return of the U.S. bases, either. Still, despite their peaceful history, if they are responsible for the Louvre massacre, they have certainly joined the ranks of their fellow terrorists in a big way."

"How did UCLAT learn of the Ocs's connection to the bombing?" Katzenelenbogen questioned. "Did someone from the Ocs movement finally contact the media to claim credit for the assault?"

"No," answered Dupont. "The connection came to our attention from an informant who regularly supplies information to a sergeant in the Gendarmerie Nationale," Calvin James grumbled. "Songbirds have a habit of singing whatever song they think will get them the most birdseed. How reliable is this informant?"

"As reliable as most who make a living turning in their fellow criminals," Dupont responded with a quick laugh. "The songbird in this case has provided reliable information in the past. He is a fairly steady customer with a fondness for French francs in large denominations. Sergeant Jouffreau believes his man is selling us the truth.

"Given the intensity of the investigation—virtually every law-enforcement organization in France is working on the Louvre disaster—Jouffreau feels his informant would not sacrifice future credibility or future earnings by fabricating lies. He thinks his man may have brought us the lead we have been searching for. I am inclined to agree."

"What made this informant think the Ocs were behind the bombing?" asked Encizo.

"He was in a bistro, when he apparently overheard a couple of Ocs supporters toasting each other over the 'wonderful step forward' made at the Louvre," Dupont said. "Hearing that tempting morsel encouraged the informant to listen for more. By the time the pair departed, our songbird says he was positive that those seeking sovereignty for Occitania had engineered the monstrous attack at the Louvre."

"So the Ocs have been implicated in the massacre," Manning related. "Unless the pair overheard by the informant gave the man their business card, there's not much we can do about it. I don't suppose they're listed in the phone directory."

Dupont shook his head. "No, but one of the pair mentioned the address of an establishment UCLAT's been watching."

McCarter drained the can of Coca-Cola he had been drinking and asked, "How's that?"

"The address belongs to a halfway house here in Paris for terrorists on the run," Dupont explained. "We have had the building under surveillance for more than two years."

"Which enables UCLAT to keep tabs on society's misfits," Katz surmised.

"Precisely," Dupont confirmed. "Which is why we have not openly acknowledged the fact that we know what the building is really being used for. But I do not mean to suggest that UCLAT has endorsed a complete hands-off policy in regard to this so-called terrorist's refuge. Far from it."

"Where do we find this home for terrorists in need of a night's lodgings?" McCarter asked.

"In the Eleventh Arrondissement," Dupont told the Briton. "Ironically, that is the same Parisian district in which Action Directe was first formed. The terrorists' refuge is in fact a privately owned bakery in a densely populated area."

"Have your surveillance teams noticed any unusual increase in traffic at the bakery lately?" James asked.

"Not particularly," replied Dupont. "If anything, fewer terrorists have been frequenting the refuge these past few days. If Ocs leftists are utilizing the facilities, then they have been very clever about it."

Katz had a question. "How many people are employed at the bakery?"

"It varies," Dupont said. "The owner and his four sons usually handle most of the baking. They do take on extra staff during the holidays, and have been known to bring in one or two extra helpers to prepare for Monday morning. Lately, however, business has been slow and the work force has been limited to the father and his sons."

"Good," commented Katz. "About the owner of the bakery...what's his reward for rolling out the welcome mat for terrorists?"

"Obviously," Dupont began, "he is sympathetic to the various causes these assorted terrorists support. However, UCLAT has also learned that the owner is compensated quite heavily for the use of the bakery's second floor. Is the fact that the owner is paid of any great significance?"

"Certainly," Katz returned. "It tells me the owner is fully aware of who he's renting space to. Now I won't feel bad if he or his boys get burned when we visit the bakery. Can you provide us with a ground plan of the building?"

"Of course," Dupont assured the Israeli. "When do you propose to initiate your probe?"

Katz answered, "We'll hit the bakery tonight."

"And see what's cooking," added Calvin James.

11

"This must be them now," guessed George Kraus from his place at the second-story window of a small automobile-repair shop a quarter block down the road from the Boulangerie Bourchat. "But perhaps not," Kraus added, changing his mind. "Only three men are getting out of the car."

Johann Becker crossed the darkened office and pulled aside the curtain next to Kraus. The corners of Becker's mouth turned upward as he studied the figures that were briefly illuminated by the glow of a streetlight. One of the three wore a hooked prosthesis at the end of his right arm. Excellent. Obergruppen-führer Zeigler's plan to lure his enemies to the bakery had succeeded.

"They are the men we have been waiting for," Becker reported.

"And the other two?" inquired Kraus. "The ones who are missing? We were told to expect five men."

Johann Becker shrugged. "All the better for us, George. This way we outnumber our foes by a ratio of four to one. They won't stand a chance."

"Which of the pigs is the Jew?" Kraus wanted to know.

"The cripple with the hook," answered Becker.

Kraus grunted in satisfaction. "Good. When it comes time to strike I will kill him."

Becker laughed. "We'd all like that honor."

An offspring of the *Lebensborn* program, founded in 1936 to produce a future generation of genetically perfect Nazis, Johann Becker had literally been bred for his role as an ODESSA officer.

Becker's mother was one of the first German women to participate in *Lebensborn*. After meeting the strict racial requirements established by the Nazis, the woman was successfully impregnated by a member of Adolph Hitler's elite SS.

Once her pregnancy was confirmed, she was transferred to the government maternity center of Klosterheide in Brandenburg. There she received the finest medical treatment Nazi Germany could offer. After her son's birth, mother and child were well provided for, residing in subsidized housing and enjoying a standard of living that scarcely reflected the dismal conditions the majority of Germans endured.

Becker was orphaned toward the end of the war and left in the care of a stranger named "Uncle Hans." In June of 1945, Hans Becker and his "nephew" fled Germany. By August of that year they had settled in Argentina.

Over the next fifteen years Johann Becker grew into manhood while undergoing his rigorous education as a student of the Reich. Becker proved an apt pupil, and if he had any regret about his past, it was that he had been born too late to help save Nazi Germany.

Deep in his heart, though, Johann Becker knew that the *Führer's* dream had not died in the ashes of the so-called Nazi defeat. Far from it. In many ways the influence of the Third Reich was stronger now than ever. And once this mission was accomplished, the Nazi dream would no longer be condemned by the lie found in history books. Becker knew that because he lived, so too lived the glory of the Reich.

"There they go," said George Kraus.

From their vantage point at the office window above the garage, the ODESSA pair watched as the one-armed Jew and his friends moved from beneath the streetlight and went to the narrow walkway leading to the side entrance of the Boulangerie Bourchat

Kraus laughed in spite of himself.

"What's so funny?" Becker asked.

"I was just thinking how strange it would be if the three men were killed inside the bakery before we had a chance to finish them off."

"They should be so lucky," Becker decided, then slapped his friend Kraus on the back. "Come. We must go below. You know how the others hate to be kept waiting when they can smell blood."

"I know, Johann. They are just like us."

12

"Come back in the morning," Claude Bourchat suggested, his protruding stomach blocking the side entrance to the Boulangerie Bourchat. "We are closed now!"

"You are mistaken, Monsieur," Yakov Katzenelenbogen corrected him, simultaneously producing his Uzi 9 mm SMG and aiming its barrel at the impossible-to-miss target of the baker's expansive waistline. "You are very much open for business. But if you disagree—" the Israeli prodded the Uzi deeper into Bourchat's flesh for emphasis "—then please tell me so at once. I'm in the mood for a little excitement."

"No," the Frenchman protested with a sickly smile, his forehead awash with a sudden outpouring of perspiration, "it is as you say. The baker is open for business. What do you want?"

"To go inside and talk," Katz said. "Unless, of course, you object."

"Never," the senior member of the Bourchat clan answered honestly, thinking that his sons would dispose of the one-armed madman and his puny weapon once they were inside the bakery.

Claude Bourchat's pipe dream lasted as long as it took David McCarter and Gary Manning to appear at

Katz's side. The former SAS commando carried his
MAC-10 Ingram machine gun with suppressor attached, while Manning was armed with his Eagle .357
Magnum.

"Who are they?" the heavyset baker asked
nervously.

"Your executioners, if you don't cooperate," replied the Israeli. "Move!"

Wondering how on earth he was ever going to get
his ass out of such a miserable mess, Bourchat complied with the order by slowly rotating his obese body
until he was facing the inside of the building. The feel
of Katz's Uzi pushing into the small of his back was all
the prompting he needed to be on his way.

The aroma of baking bread filled the air as Claude
Bourchat reluctantly guided the Phoenix Force trio
down a short corridor that led to the bakery's primary work area.

The room was quite large and had a high, white
ceiling. Two wooden tables, each approximately
twenty feet long, were situated in the center of the
room. On the right side of the room sat a pair of
powerful dough-mixing machines. The left side featured storage bins with labels designating the assorted
ingredients required for baking bread, including salt,
sugar, yeast and at least five different kinds of flour.
A heated proof box was next to the row of storage
bins.

The far wall of the room was dominated by the twin
doors of an enormous oven. The doors to the oven
pulled out and were positioned five feet above the
room's cement floor. Wire racks to the left of the oven

were covered with cooling loaves. To the oven's right was a tall metal door.

Claude Bourchat's four sons were each preoccupied with various stages of baking the day's fresh bread. Two of the sons were busy chopping and shaping portions of freshly mixed dough on one of the wooden work tables. Another of the men was emptying a quantity of flour into one of the electric mixing bowls. The last son had his back turned and was removing baked loaves of bread from the oven with a long-handled peel.

With the exception of the son hovering over the polished metal bowl of the mixer—a gangly man who looked as if he had spent the past thirty years on an alternating diet of prune juice and bran—the Bourchat boys were cut from the same broad cloth as their father. When they were not hard at work risking cardiacs in the bakery, it was evident that the boys divided their time equally between eight-course repasts and too many bottles of beer.

The son dumping flour into the electric mixer was the first to notice the unexpected newcomers accompanying his father into the bakery.

Sensing that something was wrong, he let the flour sack slip from his fingers and into the mixing bowl. He started to charge, when the sight of McCarter's M-10 made him rethink his plans.

The remaining three brothers turned to see what was happening. One look was sufficient to convince them of the seriousness of their predicament.

"What...what do you want of us?" stammered Claude Bourchat. "We are a bakery, for heaven's sake, not a bank!"

"Shut up!" McCarter commanded in fluent French. "We're not here to rob you. Who do you have staying upstairs tonight?"

Bourchat's four sons exchanged ill-concealed looks of guilt as their father blurted in response, "What do you mean? My sons and I work and live here at the bakery alone. We—"

McCarter cut short the rest of the fat man's lies with a triple burst of lead from his Ingram SMG. The noise-suppressed shots leapt across the room and into the sides of the storage bins to his left. Salt, sugar and a trickle of whole-wheat flour streamed onto the floor.

"Next time it's your face," warned McCarter, his voice etched with enough menace to back up his threat. "I asked you a question. Who's staying upstairs this evening?"

Claude Bourchat reswallowed a piece of his garlicky sausage dinner that had jumped to the back of his throat. "Tonight only five men. Five men, I swear."

"Are they armed?" asked Katz.

The elder Bourchat hesitated. "I imagine perhaps that they..."

The Israeli raised the Uzi's barrel so it was pointed directly at the overweight baker's round pug nose. "Well?"

"Yes, of course they are armed." Bourchat spat out his answer. "They would be crazy not to be!"

"Right," McCarter said, glancing at the door to the right of the oven. "What's through the door?"

The baker stared unblinking at the business end of Katz's Uzi. "The stairway to the second floor."

"Any other ways to go up or down?" the Briton demanded.

The older Bourchat shook his head. "Not unless they climb from a window or escape through the attic to the roof."

In which case Encizo and James or Dupont and the men of his UCLAT surveillance team will take care of them, thought the Israeli. "One last question," Katz continued. "In the event of an emergency you must have a prearranged system for tipping off your guests. What is it? And I warn you, Bourchat. Lie to me and your neighborhood undertaker will be clearing a forest to build coffins for you and your sons. How do you signal upstairs in an emergency?"

"There is a button located behind the mixer where Jacques is standing," Bourchat confessed, his jittery eyes shifting in the direction of his skinny son. "It is hidden by the mixing bowl, two feet off the floor. We are to press the button twice in quick succession, but only if there is trouble."

"Then let's see how it works," suggested McCarter. "You've got more trouble than you can cope with on your own."

With his Ingram trained on Jacques, the Briton crossed to the electric mixer and confirmed the alarm button's location.

"All right," McCarter announced, glancing first at Jacques, then at the rest of the Bourchats, "all of you step into the proof box. Now!"

With McCarter keeping watch on the door leading upstairs, Manning and Katz herded the French baker and his four sons into the steam-heated room next to the storage bins. Given the size of father and sons, squeezing the Bourchats into the windowless room was no small feat.

The proof box was used to decrease the time required to raise bread dough, and the temperature inside was well over one hundred degrees.

"My God!" cried Claude Bourchat as Gary Manning began shutting the proof-box door. "You can't leave us in here. If we don't suffocate, we'll roast to death!"

"Would you prefer I just shot you now?" Katz asked. The baker stopped complaining. The Israeli looked to Manning and the Canadian slammed the door closed, locking it into place.

"What was he bitching about?" Manning asked in English. "Did he miss his two o'clock feeding?"

"He was afraid he would suffocate in the hot box," the Phoenix Force unit commander said.

"Hey!" McCarter called anxiously from across the room. "What about this alarm button?"

"Take it easy, McCarter," said Manning. "I can hear your fingers itching from here!"

"Well?" McCarter insisted, poised over the button.

Yakov Katzenelenbogen sighed. "Push it."

McCarter did. Twice.

13

"Merde!" shouted an instantly wideawake Antoine Gaillac. "The alarm!"

Gaillac reached for the Ruger P-85 9 mm autopistol stashed under his pillow as Joseph Cottin rushed to the small window overlooking the street in front of the bakery.

"What is it?" Richard De Fraeye demanded, slipping into his pants and pulling a T-shirt over his head. "The police?"

"I don't see anything," Cottin reported. "One car and that's it."

"Well, Bourchat didn't warn us for the hell of it." Marc Rapagnol fed a full magazine of thirty-two rounds into his MP-40 submachine gun. "We've got trouble!"

Charles LeRiche grabbed his Heckler and Koch P9S .45 and ran barefoot to the door leading from their room. "I don't hear anybody coming up the stairs," he said as he gently opened the door. "Maybe Bourchat's just trying to scare us."

Richard De Fraeye wrapped his hand around his trusted Benelli Model 9 mm autoloader. "If this is all a joke I'll kill that fat bastard."

Joseph Cottin turned from the window and ran across the room for the Austrian MPi69 SMG hanging on a hook at the head of his bed. "I don't like it. There's still no sign of anything outside but the car. We've got to get away from here."

LeRiche pulled open the door. "We can go out through the attic and onto the roof. Then it's a simple matter for us to leap to the next building."

"Don't be an idiot!" snapped Gaillac. "We take to the roof and there are snipers waiting for us and we're dead meat."

"Have it your way," LeRiche scolded, "but don't expect flowers on your grave from me." And without giving Antoine Gaillac a chance to respond, Charles LeRiche, armed with his H&K P9S, charged from the room and down the hallway toward the staircase to the attic.

"He's gone," Cottin said almost sadly.

"Piss on him!" snarled Gaillac. "He always was pigheaded. Well, now the police will be mounting that big head of his on a wall."

Marc Rapagnol looked worried. "Enough!" he commanded. "We are in agreement, then? All of us? Downstairs through the bakery?"

"There's no need to hold an election," urged an increasingly agitated Antoine Gaillac. "Hurry!"

The four French terrorists followed Gaillac from the room. As they made their way downstairs to the bakery Gaillac cautioned the others to be quiet—a useless gesture considering how much noise they were making clumping down the steps. Finally the gunman, wielding the Ruger P-85, gave up, convincing himself that this was the last time he would ever join forces with such a pack of inept amateurs.

Gaillac reached the bottom of the stairway first, and immediately he twisted the knob on the door barring his way. Whatever was waiting to greet them on the opposite side would be there whether the door was opened slowly or quickly. Gaillac preferred to do everything quickly.

The door flew open on its hinges and slammed with a bang against the side of the bakery's large oven. Gaillac and the others, their weapons in combat readiness, stampeded into the room. Their anxious eyes swept from left to right in search of Claude Bourchat and his sons. What they saw instead was a one-armed old man covering them with an Uzi SMG.

"Throw down your weapons," Yakov Katzenelenbogen ordered in no uncertain terms.

The terrorist's expression telegraphed his decision as he raised his P-85 to gun down the Phoenix Force unit commander. The killer's finger tightened around the Ruger's trigger an eye blink before the first bullet of Katz's 3-round burst made *bifteck haché* of the subgunner's heart.

The next pair of shots from the Israeli's Uzi gave the dying Frenchman a massive headache. One 9 mm parabellum slug blew his nose in a bloody reverse sneeze of mind-numbing destruction. Cartilage and bone fragments mingled with mucus and brain tissue.

The final Uzi zapper renovated the top of the terrorist's skull with a bright scarlet skylight. Blood splashed from the wound and sizzled against the doors of the bakery's oven. His body slumped against the oven and did a slow slide to the floor.

The terrorist's companions made their move at the same time. One of the killers swung his MP-40 up and over just as an explosion of agony stitched a burning path up his side.

Eyes flashing fire, the enemy gunner screamed. Swiveling toward the source of his agony, he coaxed his MP-40's trigger to life.

A flurry of 9 mm slugs pelted the surface of the large metal mixing bowl behind which David McCarter had dropped for cover. The bowl, suspended on the cradle of the mixer, sang in protest as three of the submachine gun's 9 mm missles punctured the metal and kept on going.

Two of the terrorist's bullets slammed into the electric mixer's dough hooks and were deflected down and out through the bottom of the bowl. The third 9 mm Luger slug avoided the obstacle and continued on course. Only the fact that the bowl was filled with a thick mixture of unbaked bread dough prevented the bullet from completing its flight and striking McCarter in his chest.

The Englishman was waiting to use his Ingram M-10, when bullet number three, dough clinging to it like chewing gum stuck to the heel of a shoe, broke through the surface of the bowl and came very close to hitting McCarter.

"Ducks for you, mate," the Cockney commando muttered, rising from in back of the mixing bowl and finishing the job he had started with his M-10. The Briton's deadly aim sent a swarm of 9 mm death buzzing over the MPR-40 subgunner's body. Six direct hits and a single whining scream later left Mc-

Carter's bleeding target a lifeless lump of lacerated flesh.

Twin claps of .357 thunder rocked the interior of the Bourchat bakery as Gary Manning, attacking from the space between the oven and the proof box, put his Eagle to work on a Benelli-toting hoodlum. The Force's best shot with a rifle was equally as accurate with a handgun.

The terrorist shrieked bloody murder in the three languages he knew and two he obviously did not. But his message was clear. This was not a fight he would walk away from.

Blown apart at the wrist, the terrorist's severed right hand sailed through the air and onto one of the bakery's wooden work tables. The Italian-manufactured B-76 and the hoodlum's amputated hand made the trip together, striking the floured top of the table in a sudden puff of pink and white. The shocked killer clamped his left hand over the spurting stump at the end of his right arm and howled like a wolf baying at the moon. Another pair of .357s from Manning's Eagle caught him in midhowl and switched off his internal lights forever. The Magnum meteors flung the gunner on a one-way trip into oblivion. Yakov Katzenelenbogen dove below the nearest wooden table as a madman toting a MPi69 raked the bakery with a blistering stream of 9 mm parabellum rockets. A shower of splinters and bread dough rained over the Israeli commando. The attacker continued his deadly sweep of the bakery, homing in on Gary Manning.

The Canadian bravely held his ground and unleashed every ounce of the Eagle's considerable man-stopping power. Two shots did the trick, picking the gunner off his feet and ending the MPi69's free-for-all with a double dose of Magnum mayhem before any of the Austrian submachine gun's bullets could come within a foot of hitting Manning.

Great for the Canadian. Murder for Claude Bourchat and three of his sons.

The final eight rounds of the subgunner's MPi69 ripped through the flimsy exterior of the bakery's proof box. Claude Bourchat died instantly with a shot to the center of his heart. Three of his sons played host to the remaining bullets flying through the confined space of the hot box.

Only Jacques Bourchat, the brother built like a fence post, was not hit. The bullets from the terrorist's SMG did not have the energy to reach the man flattened against the far corner of the tiny cubicle.

Katz picked himself up off the floor. "Next time they'll listen when I tell them to drop their weapons," he said sardonically.

"Nice bunch of boys," said McCarter as he surveyed the bodies littering the room. "But one thing bothers me."

Katz agreed. "I count only four terrorists...."

"And baby makes five," Gary Manning said as Rafael Encizo picked that precise moment to emerge through the doorway and into the bakery with a prisoner in tow.

"Where'd you find him?" Katz questioned.

"He found me," admitted Encizo. "Seemed to think that getting the hell out here was a good idea. Caught him up on the roof."

"What happened to his head?" asked McCarter, noting the nasty cut on the side of the gunner's face. "He try to get cute?"

Encizo grinned. "I didn't know how to tell him in French to drop his gun."

McCarter nodded with understanding. "So you used body language."

"At least you didn't speak too loudly," Manning said. "Not like some people might have."

"Not anyone we know, I trust." McCarter smiled.

"Heaven forbid," the Canadian shot back.

"It's a shame about the others," Katzenelenbogen decided. "But at least we've got one prisoner. We could have come up empty-handed."

Gary Manning pointed his thumb in the direction of the bullet-riddled proof box. "What about the Dough Boys?"

Katz shrugged indifferently. "Looks to me as if they should have stuck to baking."

"Yeah," McCarter said with a laugh. "Better bread than dead."

"Come on, UCLAT can clean up the mess here," Katz said. "Let's get our prisoner someplace nice and warm where we can have a talk. Mr. Blue's going to be wondering where we are."

Encizo shoved the terrorist forward with his H&K MP-5. "Well, then, let's not keep the man waiting."

With the Phoenix team's unit commander in the lead, the five men filed out of the bakery. It was likely that occupants of the adjacent buildings had overheard the gunfight, but Edmond Dupont had reluctantly promised that no French authorities, UCLAT or otherwise, would be permitted to advance on the terrorist's hideaway until Katz gave the all-clear over the radio.

They reached the front door of the bakery and turned left to where Dupont's BMW was parked. McCarter withdrew the car keys from his pocket as they approached.

"I'll drive again," the Briton volunteered. "Who wants to ride shotgun?"

"I'd rather sit in back with Mr. Brown and the prisoner," Manning answered a little too quickly.

"Which means there won't be room for me," Yakov concluded. "So I guess that makes me copilot. But only until we pick up Mr. Blue."

"Thanks for the vote of confidence," McCarter said as he moved to the driver's side of the BMW. "It's nice to be loved."

SILENTLY, WITH ITS HEADLIGHTS OFF, the Citroën emerged from the garage. The car turned right. Two other ODESSA vehicles followed, each car containing four men.

George Kraus rode in the lead car, his Swedish M-45 SMG cradled in his lap. "I feel lucky tonight," he said, sticking the barrel of his weapon out the open window. "I smell victory in the air."

The driver of the car pushed the accelerator to the floor and the Citroën shot forward.

14

David McCarter was about to get into the BMW, when a dark black shadow moving down the street caught his attention.

"Damn!" the Briton swore. "Hit the dirt," he shouted, his instincts taking over in a desperate attempt to save his life.

Slamming the door, McCarter tensed his legs and dove headfirst over the hood of the BMW. Manning reached out and grabbed the Englishman by the shoulder, pulling hard.

The Canadian dropped to the ground, taking his British friend with him. McCarter's ankles cleared the hood of the BMW and disappeared from sight just as all hell broke loose.

Colonel Yakov Katzenelenbogen and Rafael Encizo reacted just as quickly to the danger rushing their way. Knowing they were finished if they remained upright, the Phoenix Force pros threw themselves to the unyielding sidewalk. Encizo slowed down only long enough to try to drag their prisoner to safety.

Unaware of what his captors were doing, the French terrorist resisted, mistakenly believing that the time was ripe for him to try to escape. Swinging his arm as hard as he could, the killer broke free of Encizo's grasp and started to run. He reconsidered his plans after the first of more than a dozen 9 mm parabellum bullets started cutting him to ribbons. A millisecond later the Frenchman had nothing to reconsider with.

The terrorist's final act in life, a sharp intake of breath sounding like a scream in reverse, was lost in the brutal barrage of submachine gunfire. The BMW's windshield was destroyed as a spray of metal cracked and spiderwebbed the glass. Bullets punctured the car's body bumper to bumper. Then the lead Citroën was past the bakery and whizzing down the street.

Katzenelenbogen lifted himself to his left elbow just as the second Citroën raced into view.

"Down!" Katz shouted, flattening himself to the sidewalk again as a fresh wave of 9 mm death threatened to wash four-fifths of Phoenix Force off the face of the earth.

McCarter and Manning were plastered near the right front tire of what was fast becoming Edmond Dupont's junk heap. Encizo and Katz were a few feet away, also making like commando-style pancakes. McCarter shielded his head with his arms.

Bullets peppered the bakery building. The headlight nearest Manning exploded. Something hot tore at the collar of Encizo's coat. Katz clutched his Uzi to his chest, waiting for the opportunity to retaliate.

McCarter swore as he recognized a familiar smell. "Petrol!" he shouted.

The second Citroën zoomed by. The fox-faced Briton was not fooled. Bad things always come in threes. A hurried glance up the road showed another metal monster on wheels streaking through the darkness toward them. The smell of leaking gasoline grew stronger.

CALVIN JAMES HAD RELAXED when he saw Katz and the rest of his Phoenix Force partners emerge from the bakery. The Phoenix Force commando had listened anxiously when the shooting had started. He hated to think his colleagues were squaring off against armed opponents while so far he had kept a low profile and done nothing.

It had been Katz's suggestion that they not commit all of their available manpower to the assault on the bakery, that they hold something in reserve. The Israeli's reasoning made sense. There was a strong possibility that the tip-off regarding the bakery had been part of an elaborate plan to lure Phoenix Force into a trap. If so, the last thing they wanted to do was to leave the area outside the building unprotected.

And so James had been elected watchdog. Hiding within the shadows of a single-story menswear store at the easternmost end of the street, he had a clear view of the entire boulevard. While the shooting inside the bakery raged on, more than one individual in the neighborhood had poked his head outside for a look. But that was the extent of it. No one had been curious enough to pay a visit to the bakery to determine whether those really had been bullets they'd heard flying about.

But Calvin James was about to reinforce his reputation as a Phoenix Force warrior. The black commando went on full alert when three mystery cars raced straight for the BMW and the remaining members of Phoenix Force. A lesser man might have panicked in a similar situation, but reacting as a lesser man was not what being a member of the world's toughest counterterrorist outfit was all about. Calvin James had been handpicked to be one of the Phoenix Force superstars. He could never betray that confidence by failing to give one hundred percent of himself when the going got rough. That his friends were in danger was all the dedicated black commando needed to know.

Leaving his hiding place, James charged to the side of the road. In his right hand was a Ring Airfoil Grenade launcher. Developed by the ultrasecret Defense Advanced Research Projects Agency during the height of the Vietnam War but rarely used since, the RAG, in James's opinion, was one of the most overlooked weapons of the past two decades.

Unlike the M-79, whose 40 mm grenades follow a sharp trajectory to reach their objective, the RAG launcher could be fired like a rifle because of the aeroballistic styling of its donut-shaped projectiles. The weapon's magazine contained five 53 mm rounds.

This particular incarnation of the RAG had an effective range capability of 4,200 feet, almost 3,600 more than the Phoenix pro needed. He braced the RAG's stock against his shoulder and took aim, setting his sights on the third car in line. He fired. The resulting thump was like that of an M-79; the recoil was comparable to a 40 mm. As the ring of destruction flew to its target, James corrected his aim and fired again, this time zeroing in on the car in the lead.

Shots three and four were reserved for the car in the middle. James saved the last RAG round as a spare. Total elapsed firing time was under seven seconds.

The first 53 mm airfoiled grenade had scored a direct hit, striking its objective where hood and windshield met. Flame sprouted from the explosive impact. Glass disintegrated, blinding the vehicle's four passengers in a single blow.

A shower of shrapnel filled the Citroën's plush interior, turning the car into an instant coffin for those inside. All but one of the doomed occupants died without screaming. The driverless auto veered suddenly to the left and slammed into the bullet-riddled shell of the BMW.

JOHANN BECKER SCREAMED as the second round from Calvin James's weapon clipped the front bumper of the Citroën. Metal ruptured and the front of the car was lifted from the street in a whooshing roar of burning light. Becker ducked and shielded his eyes as the windshield imploded.

George Kraus shouted something unintelligible as the car settled back onto the street. Kraus stopped shouting. Dazed, the tops of his hands bleeding, Becker uncovered his face and turned to check on Kraus. Kraus was dead, most of his head decorated with jagged slivers of metal and glass. His tongue protruded from his mouth like a fat pink worm. Blood was everywhere. The corpse of Dieter Harz, slumped beside Kraus, was equally as mutilated.

"Hilfe." The plea for help from someone in the front seat was scarcely more than a whisper. Even as Becker turned to the sound, all life left the driver's body in a gurgling sigh.

Clasping his MP-38/40 submachine gun to his chest, Johann Becker pulled on the handle of his door and pushed it open. The ODESSA Nazi staggered from the car, the reality of his apparent defeat more stinging to his senses than the acrid smoke burning his eyes.

Trapped between the shattered remains of the other automobiles, the Germans riding in the middle Citroën had no time to respond to what was happening before it was happening to them, too. A double RAG salvo struck the French touring car in side-by-side hits. The twin explosions transformed the Citroën's interior into an inescapable meat-grinding monster. Shredded flesh melted into the upholstery. Part of a burning arm fell like a grisly torch onto the street.

CALVIN JAMES SAW Katz, Encizo and Manning clear the wreckage of Dupont's BMW just as its fuel tank ignited with a ground-rumbling roar. The force of the blast hurled the three Phoenix commandos off their feet. A bright red-and-orange fireball rolled skyward.

The black Phoenix Force pro was seventy feet from the remains of the lead Citroën when one of its occupants stepped into view. The gunner saw James and swore in German.

Desperately the German swung his MP-38/40 up and over, determined at least to eliminate one last enemy while he still had the strength. He curled his finger around the German SMG's trigger and squeezed.

Calvin James snapped the RAG launcher into play, firing from his hip. The final 53 mm round flew from the weapon with a solid thump. The Phoenix pro's aim was true, and the donut-shaped grenade hit the gunner square in the center of his chest.

The German was dead before the explosion from the strike could reach James's ear. One second the killer was there. The next he was gone, rocketing into the void of death in a fiery trail of flame. A lone button separated from the conflagration and shot through the air like a miniature comet.

The Phoenix commando continued walking up the street as Katz and the others approached. James was relieved to see that all his friends had survived the attack. Together the men of Phoenix Force met at the place where the last German had died.

"You guys okay?" James asked.

"Fine," Katz answered. "You?"

"The same," James told him. "You were right about the bakery. The whole damn business was a sucker play." He turned to Encizo. "I saw your prisoner go down."

The Cuban shrugged. "And before we could get a single shred of useful information."

Manning pointed to what was left of the destroyed Citroëns. "So who were these characters? More Ocs?"

"Perhaps," said Katz. "Whoever they were it's too late to ask them now. Thanks for bailing us out, Calvin."

James smiled.

"What did you zap the last bastard with?" McCarter questioned. "One of the RAG rounds?"

"That's right," James returned. "I got him before he got me. There's nothing left of him."

"Hells bells," muttered McCarter.

"Yeah," said James, "a real dead ringer."

15

"Dead?" Adolf Zeigler's shock could not have been greater if he had suddenly regained the sight of his blind left eye. "All of them?" he shouted into the telephone.

"I'm afraid so," Karl Dortmann, the man Ziegler was speaking to, replied. "No survivors. Not only that, but from what I have been able to gather, that situation pretty much mirrored the one inside the bakery. All the guests were killed, including the baker and three of his sons. A fourth son managed to live and has been arrested."

"Nothing to worry about there," Zeigler stated with relief. "Neither the baker nor his sons knew of our operation." The ODESSA *Obergruppenführer* paused as he took a drink of his *Kirschwasser*. "A total loss. I still can't believe it. Surely our associates managed to strike down at least one of our enemies."

"They did liquidate one individual outside the bakery."

Zeigler's hopes soared. "Was it the one-armed Jew?"

"No," Dortmann answered with finality, casting the image of a murdered Yakov Katzenelenbogen from

Zeigler's mind. "And it wasn't any of the Jew's dangerous friends, either."

"Who, then?"

"Our associates succeeded in liquidating one of the guests from the bakery who had been taken prisoner. We think he was mistaken for one of our targets."

"Hmm," Zeigler mused. "Just as well. Prisoners have a notorious habit of talking. Not that he would have had that much to tell. Which Frenchman was it?"

"LeRiche."

"A regular hothead," Zeigler, who had familiarized himself with the backgrounds of all Ocs operatives being manipulated by ODESSA, decided. "It's for the best, then, that the liquidation took place. Enough has gone wrong for us already."

Dortmann hesitated. "Does that mean that we are not to proceed with our previous plans as scheduled?"

"Of course not!" Zeigler snapped. "The problem in Paris represents a temporary setback, but only with regard to what we had functioning in the north. Those operations will be placed on hold, but only for the time being. No, proceed as planned. Ultimately it's going to take something like this to get the French government to bow to our demands. Is there anything else I should know?"

Karl Dortmann told his superior there was not.

"Very well," Zeigler returned. "Good luck with your project."

"Thank you. I'll let you know when we have finished the job."

"You won't have to," Zeigler declared.

EDMOND DUPONT GREETED the five men of Phoenix Force as they filed into the UCLAT conference room. "I trust all of you benefited from a decent night's rest?"

"Sure. Not having someone trying to gun me down always helps me sleep better," admitted Calvin James.

"And seeing how much of that has been going on since we arrived," added Manning, "a six-hour stretch without bullets and bodies has been pretty refreshing."

"Pleased to hear it," Dupont said. "Now about last night..."

"Do you know who the men in the three Citroëns were?" Katz asked.

The UCLAT agent shook his head. "All we have determined at this point is that they were somehow connected with the Oc terrorists you confronted in the bakery."

"Which doesn't necessarily mean the guys in the Citroëns were Ocs," Encizo concluded. "Has UCLAT managed to make a positive identification of any of the twelve?"

"We're still working on it," Dupont answered.

"How about Bourchat's son?" McCarter questioned. "Has he been able to shed any light on this mess?"

"We interrogated Jacques Bourchat all night," Dupont said, "but his knowledge of what's been going on seems limited to the fact that the bakery was used as a sanctuary for various left-wing organizations. Beyond that, Jacques Bourchat hasn't told us anything we didn't already know."

"Which isn't a whole hell of a lot," James complained.

"We do know the Oc supporters hiding out at the bakery were essentially sacrificed to lure us into a trap," Katz stated. "Quite frankly, I can't see other Oc sympathizers setting up their friends like that."

"Interesting," Dupont offered. "What you're saying is that there may be another group involved who's totally independent of the Ocs?"

"That's it," Katz said. "And I would guess that this unknown outfit is the real culprit behind the massacre at the Louvre and everything else. I'm not suggesting we exonerate the Oc supporters altogether. Obviously they've had a hand in all the bloodshed since Friday night. But I think that the Oc membership is being manipulated by this other organization and they aren't aware of it."

"Which, if it's true," said Gary Manning, "puts us in an awkward position."

"Oh?" Dupont quizzically raised an eyebrow.

"It's like this," the Canadian continued. "If the only link to our investigation lies with members of Ocs, and if these members are in the dark as to who is really pulling their strings, then chasing them all over Paris isn't going to do us much good. Even if we do catch some of them, the odds are they won't be able to tell us what we need to know."

"Which brings us full circle." Dupont turned his palms upward. "If the Ocs are the only link to the group manipulating them, then you have no choice but to keep looking until you discover someone within their movement who possesses the information you require."

"That could take forever," Manning said. "And right now time's not a premium we can afford. If the

Ocs or anybody else were willing to pull off the murderous attack on the Louvre, then it's likely they have something just as rotten tucked up their sleeves. What we have to do is get to the heart of the Ocs movement and take it from there. Where are the Ocs headquartered in France? I'm assuming it's not here in Paris.''

Dupont turned to the wall behind him and pulled down a map of France. "The Ocs don't actually have a single base of operations," he informed them. "That would make it too easy for us to keep tabs on them. But the activities we know they've been involved in, for the most part, have all taken place in the southern part of the country. This makes sense because the Ocs consider the south theirs, anyway."

Encizo indicated the map. "Where in the south would you look for Ocs's headquarters?"

Dupont pointed to the map as he replied. "I'd look here, here and here. But I'm not really the man you should talk to. Your best bet would be to get together with an UCLAT operative of ours in the south. He's much better qualified to fill you in on the comings and goings of the Ocs."

"How's that?" Katz asked.

"François Audouy is an Ocs sympathizer," Dupont said. "He's not actually a card-carrying member, but he does have leanings in that direction."

"So why's he a member of UCLAT if he feels that way?" James asked.

"He's a good man," Dupont responded. "Audouy doesn't let his personal beliefs get in the way of his job. He's always exhibited the finest attitude possible when it comes to his work with UCLAT. If you want to learn more about Ocs, then Audouy is the man to see."

"What's it take for us to set up a meeting?" Gary Manning wanted to know.

"I can have you in the air within the hour," Dupont promised. "Audouy can meet you at the airport."

"Sounds as if we're going to take a plane ride, then," Katz said reluctantly. The Phoenix Force commander's aversion to flying was almost as strong as McCarter's dislike of any cigarette other than a Player's.

"Where does this François Audouy live?" James asked.

Dupont pointed on the map to a city in the south of France. "Right here. Let's hope, gentlemen, that Audouy is able to provide the information you desire."

"Let's put it this way, mate," McCarter said, noting the city on the map next to Dupont's finger. "At this stage of the game…what have we got Toulouse?"

16

Katz asked his question as soon as they were on the road and driving away from Toulouse Airport. "What can you tell us about Ocs?"

"For starters, you're not going to find him pulling a cart," François Audouy answered in an accent more reminiscent of Southern California than southern France.

"Bloody hell!" McCarter commented to Gary Manning. "He's a rarity—a Frenchman with a sense of humor."

"If you're French," James interjected, "then how come you sound as if you just stepped off the boat from L.A.? If you don't mind my asking?"

Audouy lifted his right hand from the steering wheel in a short upswinging wave. "Not at all. I was born in Toulouse. My father's French. My mother is English. They were divorced when I was four and a half. After that, Mom and I went to England to live."

"Which part?" McCarter asked, curious.

"Collier Row. It's a suburb of Romford."

"Sure," McCarter said, I know Romford. But that doesn't explain why you sound like a Yank. Up Romford way you should've come out sounding a bit like me."

"No doubt I would have," Audouy went on, "but a couple years later Mom remarried."

"An American from California," guessed James.

"Bingo!" Audouy announced. "So we moved to the States. In the span of two years I went from Frog to Cockney to Yank. By the end of the third grade it was impossible from hearing me speak to say where I'd really been born."

"So how'd you wind up back in Toulouse?" Encizo asked.

"When I got out of high school the big thing to do was discover your roots. While I was growing up I'd returned to France from time to time for visits, but nothing approaching an extended stay. When I graduated I decided to come for the whole summer.

"I liked what I saw, especially after the kind of constant tension that seems to permeate Los Angeles. The long and the short of it is that I decided to make Toulouse my home. I wound up attending college here and eventually joined UCLAT." He glanced at Katz. "But you were wondering about the Ocs."

"That's right," Katz said. "How much did Edmond Dupont tell you about our suspicions?"

"Just that you believe the Ocs may be responsible for what happened at the Louvre last Friday night, and that you feel there's a high probability that another group is really pulling the strings. A fair summation?"

The Israeli colonel said that it was. "Dupont informed us that you were sympathetic to the Ocs's beliefs."

"Not to terrorist acts such as the bombing of the Louvre, if that's what you mean," Audouy countered. "From what I've been told no one's really come forward to claim the prize for that one. It might be the Ocs. It might not. I don't know. What I do know is that I'm all for most of what the Ocs are trying to achieve.

"For years the French government has bled the south dry of its natural resources so the northeners can live the high life without doing their fair share of the work. The stunts the government has pulled under the guise of doing what's best for all the people are not unlike some of the tricks they've resorted to on an international level."

Audouy jerked his thumb toward McCarter. "Take the United Kingdom for example. Tell me, Mr. Black, what was the British dairy industry like before England joined the Common Market?"

"The absolute best," the Briton answered honestly. "There was plenty of product for everyone, at an affordable price."

"Exactly." Audouy nodded. "And what about after Great Britain entered the EEC?"

"In order to make room for foreign exports, those from France in particular," McCarter stated, "the British dairy farmers were forced to slaughter their herds. Now there's a shortage of dairy-related products in England, and what is available costs too much. If you want something as extravagant as a steak for dinner, it practically takes an act of parliament and a credit application to get one."

"Which illustrates perfectly what the Ocs have put up with from the French government for centuries," Audouy said.

"And all the Ocs want is for the south to secede from the north, forming its own country," Katz concluded.

"And they call this new country 'Occitania,'" James recalled.

"Exactly," Audouy said. "Independence from France has always been the dream of the Ocs movement."

"Edmond Dupont told us that traditionally the Ocs have always sought to achieve the creation of Occitania through political channels," Encizo informed Audouy. "Dupont had no recollection of the Ocs turning to violent measures to further their cause."

"And Dupont's right," Audouy said, agreeing with the assessment of Ocs-related hostilities. "I've lived here for more than fifteen years and I've never heard of any Oc supporters taking up arms and killing innocent people."

"But, then, you aren't a card-carrying member of the Ocs Party, are you?" Encizo pointed out.

"It doesn't actually work that way," Audouy told the Cuban, "but you're partially right. Although I am sympathetic with what the Ocs want, I'm not exactly what you would call a fanatic about it. It's just that knowing how people in the south of France are being ripped off by the north, I can understand their desire to establish their own country."

"Which could be why this shadow organization we're trying to locate got interested in the Ocs in the first place," Katz said.

Audouy glanced at the Israeli. "How's that?"

"Well," the Israeli replied, "perhaps the Ocs aren't the only ones who would like a country of their own."

ADOLF ZEIGLER AWOKE with a start, his face drenched in a cold sweat, his bed clothes clinging to his body. The ODESSA general placed a hand over his breast and took a long deep breath. His heart was thumping like a pressure cooker ready to explode.

Zeigler had experienced nightmares before. He was used to them. But never one so vivid, so disturbingly real. He rolled onto his side and reached for the glass of water on the stand next to the bed. The tepid fluid was delicious.

He set the glass down and placed his head on the pillow. The clock on the nightstand showed it was ten after nine in the morning. Schmidt had let him sleep late. Otherwise he would not have had the dream.

He'd been sitting in his favorite leather armchair, sipping a brandy. His feet were propped up on the ottoman and the pile of logs burning in the fireplace was crackling and popping. The setting made him drowsy and anxious for the comfort of his bed. His eyelids were like lead weights.

Someone behind him called his name, but when he looked to see who it was, the person was gone. He heard his name spoken again. The voice came from in front this time. Again when he looked, no one was there. He shrugged and convinced himself that he was imagining things.

"Zeigler!"

He bolted upright in his chair. The voice calling to him was mere inches from where he was sitting. Only now did he recognize the voice. He ran his tongue over his lips. They felt like sandpaper.

"Zeigler!" The voice was closer, almost whispering into his ear.

He tried to rise but could not. He was rooted to the spot. He opened his mouth and ran his tongue along his upper lip. His tongue began to bleed.

"What do you want?" he asked the owner of the voice without turning his head. "What do you want?"

"You know, Zeigler. Look at me!"

"No," he refused.

"Look at me, Zeigler! Or are you the coward I've always known you were?"

"I'm not a coward. Tell me what you want."

"Look at me and I'll tell you."

Against his will the ODESSA Nazi slowly turned his head until he faced his tormentor. "A coward, am I? Ha! So tell me, pig! What do you want?"

"Why, to finish the job I started," his tormentor said.

Which was when Colonel Yakov Katzenelenbogen had reached out with his prosthetic hook and plucked Zeigler's right eye from its socket.

Never so vivid. Never so real.

Zeigler threw back his covers and swung his legs out of bed and onto the floor. As he slipped into his silk dressing gown he wondered what the dream meant. Were the Jew and his friends thinking of paying him a visit? How could they? Such a thing was impossible. And yet, he told himself as he started down the hallway for the toilet, it might not be a bad idea to double the sentries outside and put everyone on standby alert. Not a bad idea at all.

17

Karl Dortmann surveyed the group of men before him and silently wished he could boot each and every one of their asses out the door and bring in his own recruits. It annoyed Dortmann to admit that the men were capable of handling the upcoming job. None was the type to back down from a fight. They were all brave men...brave *French* men. And that is what irritated Dortmann the most: that the men under his immediate command—sixteen inside the farmhouse and the five standing watch outside—were not German.

One of the men raised his voice to be heard above the others. "Isn't it about time we started, Moreau?"

Dortmann struck a match and lit the unfiltered Gitane dangling from the corner of his mouth. Inwardly the fifty-five-year-old Nazi cringed with disgust at being called 'Moreau.' Not only were the cretins who followed his orders French, but they thought he was French, too. For Dortmann, posing as a Frenchman represented the ultimate he could give of himself as a member of ODESSA.

"Yes," Dortmann acknowledged, exhaling a puff of smoke as he returned his book of matches to his breast pocket, "it is time we started. But before we do

I have something I would like you to hear." He unfolded a sheet of paper and began to read. "Jean-Paul Albert, Louis Boulet, Lauren Pujo," Dortmann continued, running through the names until he came to the last one on the list, "and Charles LeRiche." He held the piece of paper aloft for all the men to see. "These were men we knew and respected. They were in fact our brothers, gentle souls whose only crime was that they longed too fiercely for the time when Occitania was no longer a dream but a reality.

"These men, our slain comrades, were our friends, and yet now they are dead...killed by the same oppressive monsters in the north who have subjugated our people for centuries." Dortmann squeezed a well-timed tear from his right eye and unashamedly let it trickle down his cheek. "I tell you here and now that their deaths will not go unavenged. So long as I am able to draw a breath I will dedicate myself to eradicating our enemies. If need be, for the glory of Occitania and the honor and memory of our departed friends, I am prepared to die for our cause!"

Dortmann lifted his arms overhead, and the Frenchmen in the room leapt to their feet and cheered in a frenzy of patriotic passion. When the crowd finally calmed, Dortmann continued.

"Thank you, my friends," he said to the men as they retook their seats. "I know our fallen comrades would have been as moved by your united show of strength as I was." He paused, dabbing at his moistened eyes with a white cotton handkerchief.

"Now," he said, getting rid of the hankie, "to the business at hand. Our purpose in meeting today is to finalize the last-minute details for this evening's operation. The explosives and detonators will be trans ferred from the cellar to the vans at sunset.

"Originally we estimated that it would take us three hours to complete the drive to the pipeline, but taking into consideration the inclement weather we've been experiencing, and allowing for the icy conditions we may encounter en route, we will be departing an hour earlier than previously planned.

"Naturally we will be armed, but that doesn't mean that I'm sending you on a shooting spree. We are, after all, in the south. Our differences are not with our neighbors, but with the thieves to the north. Our primary goal is to destroy sizable portions of the natural-gas pipeline. Doing so will show the northerners that we, the citizens of Occitania, will no longer tolerate their flagrant theft of our valuable resources. Are you with me so far?"

Dortmann carefully scanned the roomful of concerned and loyal Ocs. When it became obvious there were to be no questions, the phony Frenchman grunted in satisfaction and continued.

"Good," Dortmann said. "Now we will discuss the radio-controlled—" He stopped in midsentence as what sounded like automatic weapons fire drifted in from outside.

Someone ran to a window at the front of the room to see what was the matter. *"Mon Dieu!"* the Ocs terrorist exclaimed. "We are under attack!"

LEAVING BLAGNAC AIRPORT, François Audouy followed a series of four-lane roads that ran into Toulouse. From a distance the town resembled hundreds of similarly sized communities. Although traffic was congested, Audouy had little difficulty transporting the Stony Man crew from one side of Toulouse to the other.

Once out of town they followed a flat highway, bordered on either side by low hills, that passed through an assortment of small towns and villages. Many individual farms dotted the landscape.

"So how much did Dupont tell you about us?" a curious Calvin James asked.

Audouy laughed. "Not much, except to say I shouldn't let you drive my 4x4."

"Nice guy," James grumbled.

"I knew there was something I liked about Dupont," Manning said.

"Besides the warning about Mr. Blue's driving habits," added Aduouy, "Edmond Dupont also told me not to make the mistake of underestimating you guys. He admitted that's what he did. Confidentially, he felt pretty much like an ass after he saw you in action."

Katz glanced out his window, catching a glimpse of the Garrone River. Clusters of cypress trees surrounded some of the farms he saw. Other trees he recognized included a small twisted type of oak called *chêne vert*. Even though it was winter, the branches of the oak were still bearing leaves.

"What can you tell us about this farm you're taking us to?" the Israeli questioned, turning away from his window as signs posted alongside the road announced they were approaching Castelnaudry. "Has it been the site of much Oc activity?"

"Nothing to write home about," Audouy said. "Sure, some of those supporting the cause get together at the place from time to time, but it's far from being a haven for terrorists. Still, when Dupont gave me the details on what happened in Paris and how the Ocs had been implicated, the farm was the first place I thought of. Its size and natural seclusion make it an ideal location for the base of operations for some under-the-table outfit."

"How many roads in and out?" Encizo asked.

"Just the one," Audouy replied. "If something screwy is going on at the farm, no one will be able to leave as long as we're in control of the road. And if it happens that we've made the trip for nothing, then all we'll do once we reach the property is to hang a U and head back the way we came."

Castelnaudary proved to be a charming old town with numerous gray-stone and beige-plastered houses. Audouy handled the sharp turns down the narrow streets with ease. To their right was a small lake—obviously a popular spot, considering the many sailboats anchored along its shores.

With Castelnaudary behind them, Audouy followed a two-lane country road as the terrain became hillier. Tiny villages sat on hilltops in the distance. In some instances, trees jutted up against the road to provide shade for drivers in the summer.

A half hour later they came to the Aude River and the town of Limoux. Ancient stone bridges spanned the Aude. Large boulders lined the banks as a protection for when the water ran high. *Paysans*, stooped and weather-beaten, wearing blue denim working clothes and black berets, went about their business. More than one of the rotund workers sported what Audouy referred as a "wine belly."

Past Limoux the roads became even narrower. Empty vineyards were everywhere, as were one barren hill after another. Finally Audouy slowed his Toyota FJ-55 and pulled onto a dirt path leading up to the hills. It was just wide enough for them to drive on. Audouy stopped the vehicle below the top of the second hill they came to.

"This is it," he said, switching off the engine and setting the parking brake. "The farm is just over this hill. I think we should take a look to see if anything's going on before we go the rest of the way."

"No sense showing our hand before we have to," James agreed, climbing outside. Immediately a gust of winter wind whipped across the back of his neck. "Damn, it's cold out here!" He slipped his Colt Commander from its holster and told his friends, "Sit tight. I'll see what we're up against. No sense in all of us freezing our backsides off."

The Phoenix Force commando turned and silently made his way the less than fifty feet to the crest of the hill. As James neared the top he lowered himself into a crouch, until he was practically on his hands and knees when he reached the hill's summit. Thirty seconds later he was rushing back to the Toyota Land Cruiser, the expression on his face telling everyone within the 4x4 that something was up.

"What's the good word?" Gary Manning asked as soon as James returned.

"Pay dirt," James said. "I don't know how many Ocs are camped inside the farmhouse, but I counted four armed guards outside."

A rifle cracked and the 4x4's right front headlight exploded.

"Make that five!" Calvin James amended.

18

Calvin James rushed to the right as a second bullet kicked up the dirt at his heels. The black commando's actions provided a momentary diversion that the rest of the men inside the FJ-55 were quick to use to their advantage.

The doors to Audouy's 4x4 burst open. The French-born, English-speaking UCLAT agent was the first out of the truck, an N-Frame Smith and Wesson Model 629 clutched in his fist. The manner in which he gripped the .44 Magnum left no doubt that he knew how to use it.

Katzenelenbogen and McCarter followed Audouy, while Encizo and Manning made their exits from the opposite side of the vehicle. Each had their weapon of preference drawn and ready.

The sniper fired what had to be a French MAS assault rifle a third time, and once again missed his target. But the gunner's abysmally poor marksmanship was only the beginning of his problems. No sooner had the thug began shooting than he suddenly had more targets than he knew what to do with.

David McCarter charged up the hill just as the Oc terrorist corrected his aim for yet another stubborn try at bagging James the hard way. The M-10 in the Briton's hands came to life. The vulnerable clump of weeds that shielded the gunner was blitzed to shreds by four 9 mm rounds.

The terrorist screamed and flung his hands into the air, sending his MAS assault rifle flying. Pain washed over his body as though he were swimming in hot grease. Two bullets from McCarter's Big Mac slammed into the Frenchman's gut with the ease of a concrete slab going through a pane of glass. Blood pumped from the uncorked holes in his flesh and washed the ground.

Shot number three from the Ingram SMG tore apart the gunner's deltoid and scattered grisly chunks of the muscle in all the wrong places. The last round catching him shattered his sternum with a sickening crack and proceeded to churn his chest to a bloody mess laced with slivers of bone.

The French thug was flopping around like a goldfish out of its bowl, when McCarter ran into view. The terrorist opened his mouth to speak, but all that came out was a long wet hiss. He arched his back off of the ground and started to gurgle.

"Think they noticed the shooting?" Gary Manning asked, joining McCarter.

The Englishman glanced down to the opposite side of the hill, where four armed guards were racing one another to reach the top. The Frenchman in the lead raised his Belgian FNC-Model 11 assault rifle to his hip and unleashed a hastily triggered 3-round burst. The weeds next to McCarter fluttered to the ground.

"Yeah, they noticed," McCarter barked, swinging his M-18 around and down to bear on the advancing guard. "Too bad for them."

Before the guard with the Model 11 could fire again, McCarter and Manning cut loose with some well-placed shots of their own. The guard in the lead dropped out of the race with an egg from Manning's Eagle plastered across his face. Guard and Model 11 assault rifle toppled backward in a sudden spray of red.

David McCarter's telling accuracy took care of the next guard in line, this one wielding an H&K 53. One of the Ingram's 9 mm slugs struck the terrorist's right kneecap, instantly causing the man to forget totally about where he was and what he was supposed to be doing. He flung his Heckler and Koch away as though it were burning his fingers, and bent over to soothe the bloody pulp of his gunshot knee.

His head was tilting down when another Ingram invader drilled him through the top of his skull and burrowed a burning path to his stomach. The meal proved indigestable.

Gary Manning's .357 barked twice, and guard number three lost all interest in life as the Eagle's Magnums made mincemeat of the Oc terrorist's chest. Guard number four perished when a trio of McCarter's M-10 bullets played connect-the-dots with the man's eyes. The armed corpse slumped to the ground and began rolling back down the hill.

"Shit!" Calvin James swore as he joined McCarter and Manning and quickly surveyed the damage they had wrought. "Don't tell me you guys didn't save any of the fun stuff for me."

At the bottom of the hill the front door to the farmhouse slammed open and a stream of Oc terrorists began pouring out.

"Go ahead, mate." McCarter pointed toward the newcomers. "We're not greedy. They're all yours."

"How can I ever thank you," James wondered

"You'll find a way," returned the Englishman.

The Toyota FJ-55's engine roared to life, and François Audouy and the 4x4 charged up the hill. Katz rode in the front seat beside the UCLAT agent, while Encizo steadied himself as he hung out the forward door on the shotgun side of the truck. The Cuban's MP-5 was poised and ready for the trouble they were sure to encounter.

"Climb aboard!" Audouy shouted to James and the others as the Toyota gained the crest of the hill. "Let's take the easy way down!"

"Beats the hell out of walking," agreed Manning, and the big Canadian leapt onto the 4x4's back bumper a second before Calvin James did. Both men rode with one hand holding the bars of the FJ-55's luggage rack.

McCarter was the last to climb on. The fox-faced Briton elected to ride hanging out of the rear door, directly behind Audouy.

"Home, James." McCarter slapped the roof of the 4x4 once he was secure. "And don't spare the gee-gees."

Audouy chuckled grimly and sent the Toyota up and over the rim of the hill.

Four Oc terrorists were halfway from the farmhouse to the top of the hill when the Toyota FJ-55 came barreling down the road in their direction. With McCarter and Encizo hanging from the Toyota's sides, and Gary Manning and Calvin James riding like a couple of gun-toting firemen on the 4x4's rear bumper, the metal monster on wheels was the last thing the thugs expected to see. The gunner in the lead stopped dead in his tracks and allowed his three friends to pass him. Standing out in the open, he looked like some target in a shooting gallery. There was nowhere on the hillside to hide. His friends were already fighting back as he brought his own weapon, a MAT 49 submachine gun, into play.

Seeing the four Oc terrorists raising their rifles and SMGs to fire, Audouy shouted for everyone to hang tight, then cut the Toyota's wheels hard to the right. The 4x4 lurched off the downhill road. The Ocs nearest the FJ-55 opened fire. The Toyota's wheels rolled over the bumpy terrain, bouncing the men in all directions of the compass.

An Oc bullet found and destroyed the door handle next to McCarter's hip. The British commando snarled and blasted away with his Ingram M-10. One of the enemy gunmen went down, his throat blown away by a parabellum kiss to his Adam's apple.

His hand clutching the 4x4's doorframe in a precarious grip, Rafael Encizo leaned out and put his H&K machine pistol to work. The Cuban's MP-5 chattered with noisy delight. One terrorist's career ended with a diagonal slash of murderous lead that opened his belly in a burning flash of red-hot pain. The killer lost his footing, crumpled into a ball and died.

The Oc thug next in line jumped over the body of his gutshot companion while simultaneously attempting to erase Encizo from the face of the earth with a fusillade of gunfire from his FN FAL. The Cuban commando got there first with a triple salvo of 115-

grain man-stoppers that did precisely that. The terrorist was still trying to aim his rifle when his world abruptly went cold and eternally dark.

The Toyota's front tires shot over a short rock ledge that curved upward. The 4x4 was airborne. McCarter yelled with cool excitement. The FJ-55's wheels touched down as gravity reeled the Toyota in with a bone-jarring impact.

The 4x4 left the ground again. Encizo's fingers came free of the top of the doorframe. The Cuban started to fall. Katz turned and made a grab for his friend, his left hand snapping across the car seat for the sleeve of Encizo's coat. The Phoenix pro kept falling.

The Israeli freedom fighter's hand brushed the fabric of Encizo's sleeve and closed into a fist. Katz pulled back and came away with a single useless button. By then Encizo was out the door and gone.

The Cuban's feet hit the dirt and he began to tumble, rolling head over heels after Audouy's Toyota. Weeds lashed at his body, slowing him down. Air rushed from his lungs as he rolled across a rock. His MP-5 was torn from his grasp. He threw both feet forward and dug his heels into the ground. Two more tumbles and his impromptu ride came to a welcome halt. The Cuban groaned and tried to stand.

Calvin James and Gary Manning saw Encizo take his fall, but there was nothing they could do about it. They were too busy dealing with a crazy with a MAT 49 SMG who was determined to retire two-fifths of Hal Brognola's favorite counterterrorists.

Bullets from the French subgunner chased after the Toyota as Audouy cut the 4x4's wheels to the left and

gunned the engine. James and Manning leaned out
and back, balanced on the bumper, their fingers
locked onto the Toyota's luggage rack. Both Phoenix
warriors aimed as best they could and fired.

A charging terrorist yelped with a constipated grunt
as one of Manning's shots took a .357 Magnum-sized
bite out of his inner thigh. The enemy gunman
dropped his MAT 49 and howled, his face a mask of
hideous agony. Blood gushed from a severed vein as
the gunner's fingers dabbed ineffectually at the
wound, pulling away sticky and red. His eyes rocked
skyward and stayed there.

Watching their four comrades get mowed down one
right after another convinced the twelve Oc terrorists
still alive that if they wanted to remain in that most
desirable of conditions, they would have to find
themselves some solid cover—and find it *fast*.

Two who reached that conclusion a little slower
than everyone else were trying to decide whether to
make a dash for one of the three trucks parked nearby
or double back the way they had come to the relative
safety of the farmhouse.

The unknown factor proved to be the combination
of Colonel Yakov Katzenelenbogen and his Uzi SMG.
With the passenger side of Audouy's Toyota traveling
directly in front of where the indecisive Oc terrorists
were standing, Katz extended his Uzi out the window
and put some 9 mm firepower where it would do the
most good.

The two enemy gunners had a fleeting glimpse of
the Toyota racing by before their minds told them in
plain and simple terms that they were dead. Both
bodies twitched with the dance of death as they fell.

"Good shooting!" Auduoy commented to Katz. The UCLAT agent scrunched his shoulders as an enemy bullet cut a neat hole through the FJ-55's windshield and kept on going. Audouy laughed nervously "I don't think they like us."

"Ha!" McCarter, who had heard, exclaimed "They bloody well love us!"

Audouy bypassed the three Oc transport vehicles and headed straight for the barn. The large wooden doors to the structure were latched shut, but the UCLAT operative could have cared less. Using the reinforced bumper of his Toyota as a battering ram, Audouy plowed through the closed doors with a wrenching crash.

David McCarter dove into the back seat as the FJ-55's scraping passage through the makeshift entrance slammed the Briton's door shut with an exaggerated bang. Audouy mashed his foot on the brakes. The Toyota began to fishtail. Audouy eased his foot off the pedal and rode out the slide the 4x4 was taking. The FJ-55 tilted to one side and came to a halt. McCarter kicked open his door and jumped out, his Ingram M-10 trained on the crude but effective entry Audouy had created at the front of the barn. A shadow appeared. The Briton's M-10 erupted. Sputtering doom struck the shadow and lifted the Oc terrorist behind it off his feet and onto the ground. A spasm rippled the dead man's legs.

Audouy and Katz left the Toyota from their respective sides of the vehicle. Calvin James and Gary Manning jumped down from the FJ-55's rear bumper.

"Damn!" James exclaimed. "That was some ride! Where'd you ever learn to drive like that?"

Audouy grinned. "California."

The black commando grumbled. "And Dupont had the nerve to warn you about *my* bad driving."

"How about Rafael?" asked Katz.

"Far as we can tell he survived the fall," Gary Manning supplied.

Katz nodded. "Let's hope so."

19

Dizziness overcame Encizo when he attempted to stand. His head felt like the inside of an electric blender churning gravel. The Cuban settled back onto the ground and lay still.

Gunfire sounded from the direction of the farmhouse. Encizo opened his eyes and, without really moving his head, shifted his gaze to the left just as François Audouy and his Stony Man friends in the UCLAT agent's Toyota went ripping through the closed wooden doors of the barn. The Phoenix pro glimpsed an Oc gunman charging after the 4x4. The Frenchman got as far as the gaping hole where the barn doors had been before someone inside the barn put the terrorist's lifeline on permanent hold. The gunman threw his hands into the air and sailed to the dirt.

Encizo inhaled a deep breath of frigid air. He shivered and resisted the urge to let his teeth chatter. He inhaled again and his thoughts began to clear. The wave of dizziness he was experiencing subsided to a tolerable level.

More gunfire came from the direction of the barn. The Cuban glanced from side to side, searching for his MP-5 machine pistol. The Heckler and Koch was not to be seen, which meant that it was probably farther up the hill, nearer to where he had taken the fall from the 4x4.

He tensed his muscles and prepared to try to stand again. He had to locate the missing H&K. Without the MP-5 he was dead meat if one of the Ocs singled him out for target practice.

Encizo was ready to make his move, when a noise to his left warned him to stay put. Someone was coming, approaching at a run from the farmhouse. The Cuban commando shut his eyes to miniscule slits. He held his breath and played like a corpse, sliently hoping he was not about to get the opportunity to play the role for real.

The running stopped. The automatic weapons fire in the vicinity of the farmhouse escalated to a fever pitch. Through his partially closed eyes the Cuban saw a lone Oc terrorist making his way up the hill. The French gunman carried an Armalite AR-180.

The Oc terrorist gripped his assault rifle tighter in his hands as he finally reached Encizo's still body. He kept a safe distance, studying the quiet form.

Boldly the enemy thug stepped closer and, keeping his AR-180 trained on Encizo's body, kicked the corpse none too gently in the side. Nothing happened. The Oc terrorist smiled. He walked around to get a better look, then leaned forward and pointed the barrel of his Armalite at the dead man's chest. His index finger caressed the AR-180's trigger and began to squeeze.

Faster than the gunner would have ever expected a dead man to move, the corpse was suddenly very much alive. Frantically the Oc killer pulled back on his trigger finger.

Hot lead burrowed into the earth next to Encizo's shoulder as he slapped the barrel of the AR-180 aside as it fired. The Phoenix pro's booted right foot lashed up and over, slamming hard into the Oc gunman's back and left kidney area. The terrorist gasped. The barrel of the Armalite swung back for a second bid on the Cuban's life.

Encizo rose to a sitting position, his arm lashing out, clamping around the AR-180's receiver, wrenching the weapon high and to the right as more bad news poured from its barrel. The Phoenix Force veteran extended his elbows and pushed the Armalite higher, simultaneously rising to first one knee then the other, slowly making his way to his feet.

Even as it was firing the French thug shook the Armalite violently back and forth in a maddening bid to loosen the Cuban's grip on the weapon. Stubbornly Encizo refused to let go. The subgunner swore and shook the AR-180 harder. The results were the same.

The Oc killer swore and released his finger from its repeated attack on his assault rifle's trigger. The Armalite fell silent. He grunted and sought to bring Encizo down with a lopsided kick to the Cuban's right thigh.

The terrorist's kick connected. Fresh pain shot up the length of Encizo's leg. He stumbled, his knee buckling, threatening to drop him to the ground. The Cuban found his balance and fought to seize control of the Oc's Armalite. It was no good. The Frenchman was just as determined as he was to gain control of the AR-180.

Encizo was angry. Going the tug-of-war route with the terrorist was tempting suicide. Sooner or later one of the Oc gunman's friends would intervene and that would be the end of it. Shots would ring out. The dance would be over. The Cuban commando preferred to be the one calling the tune.

Giving his opponent what he wanted, Encizo waited until the terrorist pulled back on the Armalite, and then abruptly let go. With nothing holding him in place, the thug backpeddled away in a reverse motion down the hill. The terrorist's momentum carried him into a sturdy clump of weeds that clipped him at the ankles. The Oc gunman yelled and fell to the seat of his pants, down but still maintaining his tenacious grip on the AR-180.

Encizo had no intention of letting the Frenchman get another chance to use the Armalite. The Cuban's hand dove beneath his coat and his shirt for the leather thong hanging around his neck. Attached to the thong was an A. G. Russel "CIA Letter Opener"—a fiber-glass-and-nylon knife with a thick blade.

The Cuban pulled the A. G. Russel knife free from its hiding place, then stormed in for the kill. The French thug was swinging his assault rifle around with the same idea in mind. Encizo's foot snapped forward, colliding with the AR-180. The Oc gunman's eyes went wide. The Armalite was torn from his grasp; the weapon went flying overhead, bouncing even farther down the hill.

Shaped like a dirk, the "CIA Letter Opener" was perfect when utilized for close-quarter thrusts. The Oc terrorist learned that fact the hard way as Encizo leapt on top of him and plunged the blade of the A. G. Russel through his chest and into his heart.

The enemy gunman opened his mouth. A scream lurched out of his dying throat. His eyes rolled to whites and his body began to convulse.

Satisfied, Encizo yanked the knife from the blossoming wound. The Phoenix warrior wiped the blade clean and stood. Shots rang out. A trio of bullets thumped into the French thug's already-twitching body.

Encizo turned, frowning at the sight of another Oc terrorist racing away from the farmhouse and in his direction. The gunman was less than a hundred yards away and closing fast.

Encizo feasted his eyes on where the late gunman's Armalite had come to its rest on the hillside. The AR-180 was temptingly near, but might just as well have been on the moon. To try to get to it now would put him well within range of whatever weapon the advancing terrorist was using. The odds of reaching the Armalite while still in the land of the living were nil.

The Cuban warrior gritted his teeth and began running up the hill, crouching low, his feet carrying him over the earth in a zigzag pattern designed to minimize his potential as an Oc target. Enemy lead nipped at his heels. Adrenaline surged through his veins like a waterfall forced through a garden hose.

Then Encizo saw it off to the right—his H&K MP-5 machine pistol lying in the dirt. He ran for the weapon, Oc bullets chasing him every step of the way. He dove, dropping to the ground, latching onto the MP-5 as though his fingers were coated with glue.

The Heckler and Koch wrapped in his fist, Encizo threw himself into a forward body roll. More bullets pelted the hillside around him. He came out of his roll, facing downhill, the MP-5 sputtering out a definitive message of doom to the Cuban's advancing foe.

A barrage of 9 mm parabellum hell descended upon the French terrorist. Bullets from Encizo's H&K punctured his lungs in a wheezing frenzy of white-hot agony. His gun slipped forgotten from his hands. He belched. The taste of blood and bile jumped to the back of his throat. His legs stopped working and he settled down to the ground for a long winter's nap. He went out like a light.

As soon as his target went down, Encizo leapt to his feet. Gunfire coming from the farmhouse area seemed constant. Encizo clutched the welcome feel of his MP-5 in his hands and rushed down the hillside.

20

Karl Dortmann felt as safe as a raw bratwurst ready to be lowered into a vat of cooking grease. Things were definitely not going according to plan. The farmhouse was under attack and the Ocs terrorists he commanded were not fighting worth a damn. Or perhaps they were. Maybe their dismal showing in the battlefield simply meant that their opponents were more experienced when it came to armed combat.

Regardless of the reasons, more than half of Dortmann's men had been killed by the enemy. Damn their miserable French hides, anyway. No bank vault in the world was large enough to hold the amount he would have paid right then to have a crack outfit of ODESSA troops at his side.

Dortmann pulled back from the curtained window, an expression of utter dissatisfaction on his face. At the rate the Ocs were dying, he would soon be the only man left. Then what? Was he expected to take on an entire commando team all by himself? Impossible!

He moved farther away from the window. The war outside was escalating far too rapidly. He glanced across the room to the telephone on the small table next to the wall, thinking he should try to place a call to warn Obergruppenführer Zeigler that apparently no one was invulnerable to the exploits of the men who had already caused so much trouble and concern for ODESSA in Paris.

As a ranking member of ODESSA's Nazi elite, it was Dortmann's responsibility, his duty, to inform Adolf Zeigler of the recent dire turn of events at the farmhouse. Yet Dortmann, standing less than fifteen feet from the phone, did not so much as take one step toward it.

The reason Karl Dortmann refused to contact Zeigler was simple. It was because of Adolf Zeigler that Dortmann had been assigned to spearhead the contingent of Oc terrorists operating out of the farmhouse. Dortmann had formally requested that additional ODESSA agents be ordered to accompany him; the request was denied. The job, he was told, required the talents of one ODESSA operative and no more. And so he had been forced to venture alone into this den of inept bunglers.

Adolf Zeigler had turned down his request to put fighting professionals under his command, and now Dortmann was up to his ass in dead Ocs, on the verge of paying for Zeigler's denial with his life. So be it! He did not want to die, but he was not afraid of death. And if he and all of the Ocs at the farm were killed, well, then the problem of the commando team led by the one-armed Jew would be Zeigler's.

THE BARN FEATURED TWO EXITS besides the make-shift one François Audouy had created with his Toyota FJ-55. One door was on the side of the barn facing away from the hill. The second was at the rear of the building. Both doors were secured against intruders with simple dead-bolt locks. Each of the locks showed signs of advanced stages of rust.

Animal stalls occupied a quarter of the barn's interior. All the stalls were empty and spotlessly clean. A hayloft, also bare, was overhead and above where Audouy's 4x4 was parked. A rickety ladder ran from the floor to the loft.

While David McCarter kept his Ingram M-10 trained on the hole where the barn's double doors used to be, Gary Manning tucked his .357 Eagle into its shoulder rig, then opened the Toyota's trunk. Inside was one of the Canadian's favorite weapons—a Heckler and Koch G3 SG1.

"I'll go up top and cover the area in front of the barn from the loft," Manning said, removing the H&K sniper rifle and two spare 20-round magazines from the 4x4. He dropped the extra magazines into his pocket. "Give me a few seconds to get situated before making your play for the farmhouse. From my vantage point upstairs I should be able to tag any unfriendlies I see."

His H&K G3 in hand, the Phoenix team's master sniper hurried to the ladder and started to climb. The first two rungs snapped apart before the third finally proved strong enough to support his weight. In a matter of seconds he had vanished into the loft.

Indiscriminate gunfire raked across the front of the barn, but the poorly aimed shots hit no one. Clearly the Oc terrorists were not in a rush to try a little barnstorming.

"All set!" Manning called down to them.

"This is what we'll do." Katz immediately outlined his plan. "Audouy, you and Mr. Black—" he indicated McCarter ''—will exit through the rear of the barn and head for where the Ocs have their transport vehicles stationed. Mr. Blue and I will leave by the side door and circle around front. Whichever pair gets the first chance will advance to the farmhouse. When that happens, Mr. Green will be able to assist with some cover fire from the loft. Any questions?''

There were none, and so the British commando and the UCLAT operative turned and made their way to the door at the back of the barn.

McCarter threw back the dead bolt and, positioning himself to the right of the doorframe—Audouy was on the left—nudged the door open. Hinges creaked. No Oc bullets slammed into the door. McCarter leaned far enough around to glimpse out the doorway. The skeletal remains of an off-season vineyard was all that he saw; there were no terrorists in view.

''How's it look from your side?'' he quietly asked Audouy.

''All clear from here,'' came the UCLAT agent's reply.

''That's good enough for me, mate. Let's go.''

His Ingram MAC-10 held in readiness, McCarter slipped through the doorway and into the open air. Audouy followed an instant later, the comforting feel of his .44 Magnum Smith and Wesson Model 629 clamped in his fist.

Both men moved silently along the back wall of the barn, McCarter taking the lead. Icy wind slapped against their faces. The smell of snow was in the air. McCarter reached the corner of the building and stopped, letting his M-10 hang by its lanyard, tilting his head slightly forward and listening. A cold smile played across his lips.

Cautioning Audouy to remain silent, the London East-ender mentally began counting from one to five. He made it only to four before the head of an Oc gunman came peeking around the corner of the barn.

The killer's left eye widened in shock as McCarter's hands lashed forward, his fingers digging like fishhooks into the French terrorist's shoulders. The Briton pulled, dragging the Oc thug in a swift-swinging arc that ended when McCarter slammed the man into the barn's outer wall.

The stunned terrorist growled as the impact of the collision rattled his bones and nerves from head to toe. His grip tightened on the butt of his Sig Sauer P-220, but before he could get off a shot, Audouy smashed him on the side of the head with his Model 629. The skull made a crunching noise and McCarter allowed the dead-on-his-feet terrorist to drop to the ground.

"That's one way to keep 'em down on the farm," muttered McCarter.

Yakov Katzenelenbogen and Calvin James had reached the barn's side door as McCarter and Audouy exited through the rear entrance. Katz pushed open the door with the end of his three-pronged prosthesis Wind caught the door after only a few inches and opened it the rest of the way with a gentle creak of rusted hinges. Immediately a trio of bullets from an overanxious Oc gunner plowed into the doorframe.

"Looks as if they were expecting us," James said.

From the loft came the sound of Gary Manning cutting loose with a solitary shot from his G-3 sniper rifle. Manning shouted down as soon as he fired, "Your door's open. I think I got him!"

More Oc weapons were unleased in retaliation—not at the door near Katz and James, but in the direction of the loft. The Israeli and American used the opportunity to slip from the barn, turning quickly to the right. Katz and his Uzi led the way, ever ready for the unexpected.

One hundred feet from where they stood, the two Phoenix warriors could see the body of an Oc terrorist slumped on the ground at the base of a bay tree—evidence of the accuracy of Manning's sniping. Katz and James continued to the corner of the barn.

The Israeli stopped and ventured a glimpse around the corner. The Ocs's three heavy transport vehicles were lined in a row to the right of the barn. All three trucks faced the farmhouse.

None of the living terrorists was visible, but it was obvious from the noise of the gunfire that the remaining Ocs were using the three trucks for cover. Katz withdrew and quickly relayed the information to James.

"How do you want to work it?" James asked.

"David and Audouy have probably had time to get this far on their side of the barn. The Ocs are concentrating their attention on Manning in the loft."

"So maybe we can smoke 'em out in the open," James suggested.

"Right," Katz said. "And catch them in a three-way stranglehold. If they honestly think we pose a threat, they'll have to show themselves, either to us or the others. That's when we take them out."

"I'm game," James told the Israeli commando. "Come on."

Firing his Uzi as he ran, Katz sent a stream of 9 mm projectiles at the trucks. A tire was hit and exploded with an ear-aching boom. An Oc gunman concealed behind the truck reacted to the harmless blast by leaping to his feet. Two paces into his panicked flight Manning brought him crashing to the dirt with a through-and-through blast from the H&K G3.

Calvin James, standing ten feet behind Katz, fired twice with his Colt Commander at the exposed face of an Oc killer who popped up and tried to get a bead on the Force's commander. The first .45 from the black commando's gun careered off the hood of truck number three with a whining spark. The black Phoenix warrior's original target took the Colt's next slug between the eyes. Blood spurted from the wound as the killer's body dropped out of sight.

Using the diversion Katz and James were creating to their advantage, McCarter and Audouy rushed for the blind side of the trio of trucks. An alert terrorist saw them coming and lurched away from the vehicle he was using for protection, swinging his FN FAL assault rifle around to bear on the advancing men. Gary Manning's G3 scratched the Oc assassin from the land of the living before either McCarter or Audouy could fire.

Then McCarter rounded the rear of the truck parked at the end of the line of vehicles. A pair of Oc killers were waiting to greet him. McCarter twisted to his left, his Ingram M-10 dicing the chest of the nearest terrorist to instant 9 mm hash.

The last killer dove for cover, successfully avoiding a wave of lead from McCarter's Ingram SMG but jumping straight into the path of a .44 Magnum slug from Audouy's Smith and Wesson. The bullet caught the doomed man with a diagonal slash across his belly, deflecting off a rib and settling into the gutshot target's stomach like a lump of burning coal. The terrorist skidded nose-first to the ground and died.

McCarter and Audouy whirled and relaxed as Katz and James joined them at the trucks.

"They all gone?" James questioned.

Audouy nodded. "That's all she wrote."

"A real short letter," McCarter said.

"So let's check out the farmhouse," Katz decided.

The four men spread out and made their way from the trucks, getting halfway to their objective when the muffled eruption of submachine gunfire came from the house. Seconds later the door at the front of the home opened slowly.

"Don't shoot!" called a voice they recognized, and then Rafael Encizo stepped outside. The handsome Cuban's face broke into a smile. "What kept you?"

Gary Manning approached from the barn. The Canadian was as relieved as everyone else to learn that Encizo had survived the fall from Audouy's Toyota.

"Thought we lost you on the hill," Manning said.

"You'll have to do better than that," joked the Cuban.

Katz turned to Encizo as they all walked toward the farmhouse. "What's inside?"

"A cellar full of enough Hexogen to boost the place into an orbit around Mars," Encizo responded. "That, plus a single dead terrorist. I entered from the back of the house and surprised him just as he was preparing to light a cigarette. He had a gun. I had this." He held up his MP-5 machine pistol. "He was too slow."

They walked through the house's front door and into the living room. A telephone was on a table set against a far wall. The body of the man Encizo had shot lay facedown on the floor. A pack of Gitanes and a book of matches were nearby, as was a Sig Sauer P-220 autoloader.

Curious, Gary Manning bent and picked up the matchbook. On its cover was a drawing of a mountain and the words, *Pic d'Esteve.*

"What do you make of this?" Manning showed the book of matches to Audouy.

"Pic d'Esteve." the UCLAT agent read the matchbook's inscription aloud. "It's a private resort high in the Pyrenees, about a four-hour drive from here. Very exclusive. Very expensive."

"Have you ever been there?" James asked.

Audouy shook his head. "Not on what I make slogging away for UCLAT," he answered.

"So how come he could afford to go there?" The black Phoenix pro pointed to the body on the floor. "I've seen better duds on winos in Chicago. What made him so special?"

"Turn him over," Katz instructed. "I want to see his face."

McCarter slipped his booted toe beneath the body's shoulder and flipped it over. Katz knelt for a brief examination, then stood.

"I think we've found the missing link to our problem with the Ocs," the Israeli informed the group.

"You know this guy?" asked Encizo.

"Yes," Katzenelenbogen said. "I have no idea what the Ocs knew him by, but his real name was Karl Dortmann."

"Dortmann?" James repeated. "Who's he with?"

Katz replied with a single word. "ODESSA."

21

Adolf Zeigler stared at the silent telephone one last time before leaving the room in a fit of anger. Holstered at the Nazi general's side was a mint-condition Luger P.O8. Zeigler had spent the better part of the past two hours contemplating whether or not to put a 9 mm parabellum bullet through the uncooperative phone.

Karl Dortmann had failed to call Zeigler to confirm that he and the Ocs were on their way to sabotage the gas pipeline running from central France to the north. It was not like Dortmann to overlook such formalities. He should have telephoned hours ago.

But the call did not come and now Ziegler was concerned, not only for Dortmann and the planned strike against the pipeline, but for the safety and security of Pic d'Esteve, as well.

ODESSA's ventures in Paris were in shambles thanks to Yakov Katzenelenbogen. In a few short days the meddlesome Jew and his maniac friends had eradicated a delicate operation that had taken months to set into motion. Did Dortmann's silence have anything to do with Katzenelenbogen?

Zeigler could not afford to wait to find out. Karl Dortmann's whereabouts and current state of health were, at the moment, unknown. That was enough to convince Zeigler that certain precautions had to be taken at once.

Although Katzenelenbogen had no reason to suspect that ODESSA's French headquarters were located at Pic d'Esteve, Zeigler knew from his past experience with the Israeli that the one-armed man was full of surprises. The ODESSA-Baader-Meinhof fiasco had proved that much. Once the Israeli came onto the scene, the carefully orchestrated plan had gone right down the toilet. ODESSA still reeled from that stinging defeat.

It was because of that incident that Zeigler had reached his decision to put everyone stationed at Pic d'Esteve on immediate alert. Zeigler would rather his men lose a little sleep than to have them caught unprepared in a surprise attack on the resort. With everyone on alert, the Nazi reasoned as he moved downstairs to where his men waited, Pic d'Esteve had nothing to fear.

Zeigler's soldiers were standing at attention as he entered the room. Including Rottenführer Schmidt, Zeigler had twenty-five of ODESSA's finest at his disposal—more than enough to protect Pic d'Esteve.

Zeigler walked briskly, the heels of his boots clicking on the tiled floor as he made his way to the head of the group. All eyes followed the Nazi as he moved. Zeigler reached the front row of men, then slowly turned until he was staring them face-to-face.

"I have reason to believe Pic d'Esteve may soon be attacked by forces hostile to ODESSA," he began, seeing no point in mincing words. "If I am correct, they are members of the same group responsible for

ODESSA's setback when we attempted to seize the NATO missile site in Germany two years ago. They are also the forces responsible for the recent cancellation of our Paris-related activities with the Ocs.

"While it has not been confirmed, I believe these same men knew what Karl Dortmann's assignment was and why he was in the south of France. His failure to contact me regarding a strike that was scheduled for tonight leads me to suspect that Dortmann is dead."

Zeigler paused, absently running a finger over the scar below the milky orb of his sightless left eye. "As remote a possibility as it may be, Pic d'Esteve could prove to be our enemy's next target. If they follow that course of action they will pay the highest price for their stupidity. Should they be foolish enough to attack Pic d'Esteve, I will expect no survivors. All the dogs are to be killed. ODESSA may have the opportunity to avenge itself against a formidable adversary. I know you won't let me down."

Zeigler leveled his stern gaze on every man in the room. "Until further notice, Pic d'Esteve will be placed on full alert. The number of guards stationed outside will be doubled. I also want foot patrols conducted within Pic d'Esteve on a regular basis. All of you are to remain armed and prepared for combat at all times. No one shall venture in or about our headquarters on his own. Everyone shall be paired with at least one other individual until I have deemed it safe enough to cancel the alert.

"If the enemy is detected," Zeigler continued, "under no circumstances is anyone to attempt to engage them on his own. Each man is to carry a two-way radio. At the first sign of the enemy, Rottenführer Schmidt, who will be monitoring all conversations, is to be notified. Anyone who deviates from these orders will be dealt with severely. You are all members of ODESSA and I expect you to conduct yourselves accordingly.

"I may be wrong about an impending attack, but if I am not then you will all be grateful in the end for having followed my instructions. Now are there any questions?"

One man, a Nazi in his late thirties, promptly raised his hand. Zeigler acknowledged the man and ordered him to step forward.

"Yes?" Zeigler demanded.

"My question is this, Obergruppenführer Zeigler, how many men are in this hostile force?"

"Five men," Zeigler answered, again seeing no point in keeping anything from his soldiers. "The commando unit I am concerned about has five men."

"Five, sir?" the ODESSA member repeated with an audible intake of breath. "Only five?"

"Correct," Zeigler offered, keenly aware of the effect this revelation had on his troops. Already several soldiers in the back row were beginning to shift uneasily from side to side. Clearly, knowing that Pic d'Esteve was being placed on alert status to accommodate a possible threat posed by five men was most disconcerting to the ODESSA Nazis gathered in the room.

In the Nazi's simple question Zeigler recognized the first seeds of dissension—something that could not be tolerated if Katzenelenbogen and his crack commando unit were to be defeated.

"We are going on full alert," Zeigler went on, "because I am wary of the talents of these five men." He indicated his useless eye and the exaggerated scar on his face. "One of their team did this to me and left me for dead. I don't fear these men I speak of, but I will never underestimate them."

The curious Nazi started to speak, then changed his mind.

"Go on," Zeigler coaxed. "You were about to say?"

The ODESSA member gulped. "Nothing, sir. It's just that if these men are so dangerous and are responsible for everything you mentioned, then—" he gulped again "—then maybe now is not the proper time and place for us to confront them. I don't wish you to misunderstand and I don't want to seem out of line, but..."

"No, not at all," Zeigler encouraged, his tone as gentle as that of a father's to his firstborn son. "What you are suggesting is that perhaps it would be better if ODESSA abandoned Pic d'Esteve for the time being until this terrible business blows over. Hmm? Is that it? And where would you have all of us go? To one of our bases in South America?"

The young Nazi's face brightened. "Why, yes! That would be an excellent idea, Obergruppenführer Zeigler. South America would be perfect!"

"I see."

Without missing a beat, the ODESSA general whipped out his Luger P.O8 and killed the Nazi with a single shot through the heart. The dying man managed to stare at his wound for a second before he sank dead to the floor with the resounding smack of flesh against tile.

Zeigler signaled to Schmidt and the body was unceremoniously dragged from the room. Calmly Adolf Zeigler reholstered his pistol and smiled at his men, his attitude after having killed a man no different to what it would be if he had swatted a fly to death.

"Now," he addressed his soldiers, "how many others feel like your comrade?"

But by then everyone else had lost the travel bug.

22

"ODESSA must be crazy if they thought they could get away with it," François Audouy, Phoenix Force's UCLAT contact, insisted.

"Yeah, well, facing reality never was one of ODESSA's stronger attributes," said Gary Manning. "If it was they would have shucked their swastikas back in the forties."

Audouy went to the refrigerator and removed six thick steaks, which he proceeded to season with a variety of spices.

"It all ties in with the conclusions we were drawing," Katz stated. "By arranging for the Ocs to create Occitania and secede from France, ODESSA would gain something it hasn't had since the Second World War."

"Like its own bloody country," McCarter said, watching attentively as Audouy prepared the steaks. "The rest of the world would see the Ocs running the show, but it would really be ODESSA pulling the strings. The Nazis must be royally cheesed off since we came into the picture."

"Which brings us to the location of ODESSA's headquarters," Calvin James reminded the group. James looked at Audouy and continued. "You mentioned that Pic d'Esteve is approximately a four-hour drive from here."

"About that." Audouy put the steaks into the oven to broil. "With the blizzard moving in so fast, though, the trip could take longer. There's no way of accurately predicting what road conditions in the Pyrenees will be like, but you can bet they'll be bad."

"So—" McCarter dismissed Audouy's travel bulletin with a wave of his hand "—I'm sure it's nothing your 4x4 can't handle. You must have chains for the tires."

"Sure," Audouy confirmed. "Not that they'll make much difference if the roads get too icy. When were you thinking of heading up there?"

"As soon as we've eaten and loaded the Toyota," Katz said.

"What?" Audouy questioned. "Just the five of you?"

"Why not?" Encizo wanted to know. "You don't think we can handle it?"

"It's not that," Audouy told the Cuban. "It's where you're planning to go. Pic d'Esteve is not some little hole in the wall with a two-car garage out front and a double-seater shithouse in back. The resort's probably got twenty or thirty rooms, a lounge, gourmet dining facilities, a game room, an après-ski bar and a parking lot large enough to accommodate all the guests."

"Is there a wall surrounding the resort?" asked Katz.

Audouy shook his head. "There's no need for one. The access road into Pic d'Esteve is difficult enough on its own. It's the only way in or out of the resort.

Anybody approaching the place would be spotted long before they arrived.''

"Unless they drove up in the middle of a blizzard without their headlights on," McCarter decided.

"You'd have to be mad to try something like that," Audouy said.

"You don't know Mr. Black," Manning pointed to his British friend. "Mad's his middle name."

"He's joking," the Briton offered as his only defense.

"Listen," Audouy said, opening the oven and flipping the steaks. "You're not even sure ODESSA is at Pic d'Esteve. The fact that a matchbook from there was discovered next to Dortmann's body doesn't necessarily mean the resort is crawling with Nazis. Dortmann could have picked the matches up anywhere."

"Or he could have picked them up at Pic d'Esteve," Katzenelenbogen countered. "And from where we stand now we can't take the chance that he didn't. ODESSA undoubtedly has some base of operations in France. Otherwise Karl Dortmann would not have turned up. It may just be that Pic d'Esteve is that base."

"Okay, so you want to check out the resort," Audouy said. "Fine. Would you be willing to wait until I can round up some of my UCLAT associates to go along with you for the ride?"

"We could," Katz answered, "but by then any ODESSA Nazis utilizing Pic d'Esteve as their base would have had ample time to relocate. If they are there, we must get to them before they can disband. From the maps we found at the farmhouse, plus the Hexogen explosives in the cellar, it appears that the

ODESSA-backed Ocs were planning on hitting the natural-gas pipeline running from the south to the north. The effects of such sabotage would have been devastating.

"Intervening when we did put that scheme to bed, but ODESSA does not give up that easily. If they want to disrupt the supply of natural gas to the north, then eventually they will find a way to do it—unless we move to stop them now.

"So I am sorry, Mr. Audouy," the Israeli apologized, "we cannot wait for more of your UCLAT compatriots to join us on our mission. You are welcome to come, if you would like. Your assistance in navigating the mountainous roads of the Pyrenees at night would be greatly appreciated. If you elect to remain behind, that is all right, too. Either way, my men and I plan on visiting Pic d'Esteve tonight."

"Then you can plan on me being there with you," Audouy said, taking the steaks from the oven. "We can load up the Toyota as soon as we've had dinner. I hope you're hungry."

McCarter laughed. "Are you kidding, mate? I could eat a bleedin' horse."

"Great!" Audouy said, putting a steak in front of McCarter. "This is your lucky night!"

23

Snow whipped against the Toyota's windshield as François Audouy and the men of Phoenix Force followed the treacherous twists and turns of the mountain road leading to Pic d'Esteve. They drove without headlights as they entered the final leg of their journey, the durable 4x4 traveling at a snail's pace along the inside lane.

Fierce winds buffeted the Toyota as they rounded another of the seemingly endless curves. The FJ-55's tires held tight to the slick surface of the roadway, the chains biting through whatever patches of ice they encountered with reassuring regularity.

Inside the Toyota driver and passengers rode in silence, each man a party to his own private thoughts. Audouy's primary concern was to safely deposit his 4x4 as near to Pic d'Esteve as possible without arousing the suspicions of the resort's occupants. Gary Manning wondered about the number of ODESSA Nazis they were likely to discover. Rafael Encizo sat quietly with his fingers tapping the frame of his H&K MP-5 machine pistol.

Calvin James closed his eyes and relaxed with a series of deep-breathing exercises. Katz hoped his plan to hit Pic d'Esteve was a good one, while David

McCarter wished only that his dinner would stay in his stomach.

One mile from their goal Audouy pulled the FJ-55 against a sheer wall of rock and parked, setting the hand brake and stopping the engine. The front of the Toyota was tilted upward at a thirty-degree angle. The sound of the wind lashing the Pyrenees had become more pronounced when the Toyota's engine was turned off.

"End of the ride, guys," Audouy said, turning on a filtered dome light so dim it would be invisible beyond the 4x4's tinted windows. "We'll hoof it the rest of the way."

"How much farther is Pic d'Esteve?" asked James.

The UCLAT agent told him, then added, "Any closer and we'd be risking detection."

"And if the ODESSA Nazis are waiting for us at the top of the hill," Manning offered, "telegraphing our arrival is the last thing we want to do."

Encizo thoughtfully observed, "If ODESSA has posted guards around the resort, they're going to be colder 'n hell. And unless they've kept moving to keep their blood circulating, their reflexes and response time to danger will be greatly diminished."

"One thing's for sure," McCarter pointed out. "In this storm we're not going to get very far by ordering them to 'freeze.'"

Manning coughed politely. "Right."

"You all know where to make your entrances after we've dealt with the resort's exterior defenses," Katz said by way of a last-minute review. "Once we have ascertained that Pic d'Esteve is definitely being utilized as an ODESSA base of operations, Mr. Blue and

I—'' the Israeli indicated James ''—will initiate the strike from the rear of the resort. That will be the signal for the rest of you to move in.''

Katz nodded to Encizo and Manning. "You two will enter through Pic d'Esteve's main lobby and work your way from one side of the building to the other. If all goes as planned, you'll be joined by Mr. Blue and me somewhere in between.''

"With both of you chasing the enemy toward us," Encizo mused. "Interesting.''

"And while the four of you are doing that," Mc-Carter said with a familiar tone of impatience, "Audouy and I will be taking a tour of the building via the kitchen. We'll also rendezvous with you somewhere inside the resort.''

"Which shouldn't be too difficult," James decided with a grin. "All you'll have to do is follow the sound of the shooting.''

"After what it's taken us to reach this place," the Briton replied, "that'll be music to my ears.''

"Well," Katz said, "the night's not getting any younger.''

"And neither are we," Manning decided. "Let's hit the road.''

Audouy killed the light and then everyone traded the reasonable warmth of the Toyota for the bitterly cold weather outside. All of the men wore UCLAT-supplied thermal one-piece action suits that were insulated with Gore-Tex and had Velcro-attached fur-lined hoods. The white camouflage outfits retained body heat without the cumbersome bulk typically associated with winter wear.

Pliant, rugged deerskin gloves and blizzard boots with molded waffle soles and heels for extra traction on ice completed their uniforms. Even so, in spite of their protection, stepping from the Toyota into the freezing reality outside the 4x4 was a jarring shock to their senses.

Wind screamed like a tortured animal. Snow swirled about them in a frigid vortex. With Katzenelenbogen and Calvin James in the lead they began to move. Manning cast a wary eye over his shoulder; ten feet into the journey the outline of the Toyota was no longer visible.

Phoenix Force had come to Pic d'Esteve expecting trouble and its members had armed themselves accordingly. Besides the Uzi SMG he usually favored, Katz also carried a Beretta Model 70-S loaded with .380 hollowpoint bullets. Calvin James's weapons included the Ring Airfoil Grenade launcher that he had successfully used in Paris, a Smith and Wesson M-76 submachine gun, his 6-96 "Boot 'n Belt" knife and his Colt Commander. A .357 Colt Python worn in a hip holster completed his armament.

McCarter's battle gear consisted of his Ingram M-10 SMG and Browning Hi-Power. As a backup piece he wore a .38 Special Charter Arms snub-nosed revolver in a holster at the small of his back.

Gary Manning carried an H&K G-3 assault rifle and .357 Magnum Eagle, while Rafael Encizo's trappings included his Heckler and Koch MP-5, an S&W Model 59 worn on his hip, and a Walther PPK using .380 caliber rounds, which rode in a shoulder rig tucked under his left arm.

The UCLAT agent was equally prepared for whatever hazards lay ahead. In addition to the S&W M-629 .44 Magnum Audouy had used during the attack on the farmhouse, he also had with him a MAT 49 SMG. All the men, including Audouy, were equipped with an assortment of grenades and spare ammunition.

Progress was slow out of necessity. Unsure of where ODESSA guards might be hiding, the group was forced to advance up the road to Pic d'Esteve with the utmost caution. The wind howled constantly, pressing against the bodies of the men like a powerful invisible wall. Tears moistened their eyes and threatened to freeze on their cheeks.

They were thirty minutes into their march when Audouy caught up to Katz and signaled for him to halt. Using a quick series of barely discernible hand gestures, the UCLAT operative informed the Israeli commando that Pic d'Esteve was around the next bend in the road.

The Phoenix Force commander indicated that he understood, then motioned for the others to continue forward. Suddenly Katz stopped and held up his left hand. Less than ten feet ahead, huddled together like bookends, a couple of armed guards stood watch, their effectiveness diminished by the fact that they were both turned away from the road with their backs to the wind.

Katz's pulse raced at the sight of the guards. That each man carried a rifle told the Israeli that Phoenix Force had indeed stumbled upon something more than an exclusive resort for wealthy ski enthusiasts. Katz gestured for James to follow, then swiftly covered the distance to where the two guards were positioned.

Like a pair of ghosts, the Israeli and the American approached their foes undetected. Given their proximity to Pic d'Esteve, using guns to eliminate the guards was out of the question. Even with the terrible noise the wind was making, it was unlikely that gunshots would go unnoticed by other guards stationed outside.

Katz and James did not need firearms to dispose of ODESSA trash. The black commando had his double-edged G-96 knife, which he noiselessly removed from its sheath under his right arm. Yakov Katzenelenbogen's silent killer was his three-pronged hooked prosthesis.

The two Phoenix Force professionals struck, simultaneously snaking arms around their opponents' necks, lifting their heads and pulling them back, exposing the flesh of vulnerable throats. The G-96 "Boot 'n Belt" and the deadly three-pronged prosthesis moved as one.

Wet gasps spilled into the night. The ODESSA duo thrashed like fish out of water. Blood spurted in a rush of steam from their wounds. Their struggles grew weaker, then vanished altogether.

Katz and James lowered the bodies to the frozen ground. The Israeli noted that one of the dead men wore a two-way radio strapped to a belt. Katz removed the device and slipped it into his pocket. Apparently the guards were in direct contact with a command center within the resort. Once the slain guards failed to respond when summoned or else did not radio in a scheduled status report, those inside Pic d'Esteve would know the resort's security had been violated.

Katz stood as Manning and the others approached; the Phoenix commander was keenly aware that time was not on their side. He tugged on James's sleeve for the American to follow, then set off up the road as fast as he dared to go.

Twenty-five yards farther on another pair of ODESSA guards were discovered. Unlike their already-dead comrades, however, these two did not have their backs turned to the wind. Not that it changed the outcome of their brief encounter with Katzenelenbogen and James.

By the time the guards realized that the shadowy figures hurrying toward them through the blizzard were not other sentries, it was already too late for either of the Nazis. One moment they were standing watch, the next they were gurgling their lives away in swift cold fits of terminal darkness.

Katz and James successfully repeated their double-or-nothing gambit against ODESSA guards three more times before they finally saw Pic d'Esteve. Built on a leveled section of rock at the foot of the road, the resort was little more than a vague outline highlighted in places by a faint yellow glow pushing through the occasional uncurtained window.

Gary Manning and Rafael Encizo separated from the group and ran across Pic d'Esteve's parking lot. More than a dozen vehicles, primarily BMWs and expensive Mercedes', occupied the area. The Canadian and the Cuban rushed to the car nearest the resort's main entrance, where they dropped to the ground and out of sight, there to await Katz's signal for the attack to begin.

In another two minutes McCarter and Audouy were similarly situated, positioned in readiness outside the door to Pic d'Esteve's kitchen. Katz and James kept circling the property, making for the rear of the resort. Before they reached their destination the speaker on the ODESSA two-way radio in Katzenelenbogen's pocket began emitting a high-pitched beeping noise.

Katz and James ran faster.

24

"Luft and Kreutz do not answer," Schmidt said, repeatedly depressing the button that should have alerted the two guards. Schmidt changed frequencies and pushed the button again. Crackling static was the only reward for his efforts. "I get no response from Durst and Reid, either, *Herr Obergruppenführer.*"

"Impossible!" Adolf Zeigler snapped, shoving Schmidt aside so he could operate the radio himself. Five channels had been allocated to the sentries posted outside, and yet none of the guards could be raised on any of them.

"This is ridiculous," Zeigler fumed, his wide palm striking the side of the radio's cabinet. "Someone has to hear us. Perhaps it is only atmospheric interference from the storm, Schmidt. Or some technical malfunction. What do you think?"

"I sincerely doubt it. The guards are too near Pic d'Esteve for the storm to ruin our signal. Besides, the radio was working perfectly fifteen minutes ago when I last checked on the men. In my estimation, there is nothing wrong with the radio, Obergruppenführer Zeigler. The reason the sentries are not answering our calls rests with them, not us."

"Bah! You're no help!" the ODESSA general concluded, the possibility that Pic d'Esteve might be under attack tying his stomach in painful knots. He rose and pointed a stern finger at the chair in front of the radio. "I don't care how you manage it, Schmidt," the Nazi said, his voice bristling with anger, "but you sit your ass down and contact the guards this instant! Do you hear?"

"*Ja.*" Schmidt nodded meekly. "I hear."

What he also heard was a series of five multiple explosions ripping across the back of the resort.

"Never mind the radio!" Zeigler shouted. "*Mein Gott,* never mind!"

JAMES EMPTIED the Ring Airfoil Grenade launcher's magazine in a side-to-side sweep lasting less than seven seconds. Five 53 mm donut-shaped projectiles flew to their target, all the RAG rounds exploding against the ODESSA stronghold in a thundering roar of unbridled destruction.

Chunks of stone and shards of glass fell from the building. Flames ignited portions of the roof and lit the sky. One ODESSA Nazi, unfortunate enough to be standing in front of a large picture window when the third RAG ring plowed through it, was vaporized in a blinding flash of bloodred heat and light. Another swastika sweetheart was crushed to death as a wall collapsed and buried his broken body beneath a quarter ton of masonry.

Calvin James unslung his RAG launcher and let it fall to the ground. "Guess you could say they know we're here."

"Something like that," Katz agreed, then charged with James into Pic d'Esteve.

The noise of the black Phoenix pro's RAG assault was music to McCarter's ears. Never content to sit on the sidelines during a battle, Stony Man's British lion flew into action the second the signal to attack was given. With Audouy following close behind, McCarter kicked open the door to Pic d'Esteve's kitchen and ran inside.

The kitchen was not empty. Two ODESSA members were preparing to investigate the disturbance caused by the first airfoil grenade explosion, when McCarter's unexpected entrance put their plans on ice.

Wielding a STEN Mark II SMG, one of the Nazis whirled and opened fire. McCarter dropped to the floor; Audouy did the same—both men narrowly avoiding the spray of metal burning up the air just over their heads. Pots and pans were torn from their hooks. A punctured pipe started hissing steam.

The other Nazi rushed around a long wooden butcher's table, an H&K VP-70Z 9 mm pistol locked in the fist of his right hand. McCarter saw him coming and rolled out of the way of a barrage of bullets. Audouy escaped by twisting in the opposite direction.

McCarter came out of his roll. He sat up, his M-10 Ingram chattering to life at the exact moment the Nazi gunner was being measured for his coffin. Slugs from the Briton's big Mac peppered the man's chest with lead. The damage from the Nazi's point of view was nothing to sneeze at.

Two M-10 crunchers blasted the ODESSA gunman's heart apart as if it were a hard-boiled egg struck by lightning. Another couple of rounds transformed the killer's lungs into a sieve of despair. The Nazi gunner sent his VP-70Z on an unscheduled flight across the kitchen, then doubled over in a perfect imitation of a dead man.

The first Nazi gunner watched his partner's swan song long enough for Audouy to get into the act with his Smith and Wesson Model 629. The UCLAT agent fired twice, each of his .44 Magnum payloads catching the gunman at the wrong end of a universe of pain.

Screaming bloody murder that he was hit, the ODESSA Nazi did the agony waltz around the kitchen, his STEN Mark II a forgotten relic as he flapped his arms up and down. Shot in the hip and across his left side, he took one look at the rubbery tube of intestine bulging from his wound and died.

"Lousy Fighter," Audouy commented as he climbed to his feet.

"Yeah," McCarter noted with a sardonic laugh. "No stomach for it."

Encizo and Manning entered Pic d'Esteve via the large double doors opening onto the lobby. Four ODESSA Nazis were waiting to greet the Phoenix Force superstars. The first was at the reservation desk. Two more ODESSA gunners occupied the territory in the center of the room, while the fourth was at the bottom of the staircase leading to the second floor. All but the killer playing desk clerk were armed with MP-40 submachine guns. The clerk's choice of weapon was an Ithaca M-51 autoloading shotgun.

The Nazi at the desk reacted to the Phoenix Force duo's appearance by bringing his M-51 to bear on the Canadian and the Cuban. Manning lined up the G-3 assault rifle he was holding with the thug's midsection and cut loose with a full six rounds of Nazi-hating .223 Remington slugs. The 5.56x 4 mm projectiles sliced across the shotgunner's belly with less than surgical precision.

The ODESSA killer screamed, his finger jerking back on the Ithaca's trigger. The M-51 boomed. A load of 00 buckshot gored a section of the lobby wall. His face turned a deathly white color. Blood seeped from his gut in too many places.

The gunner twisted, falling to his knees, aiming his Ithaca to the side. His finger pulled on the trigger again, unleashing another round—this one striking a comrade and lifting the ODESSA gunman off his feet like a human comet. A sticky red trail was left behind. The desk clerk and his friend each checked out of Pic d'Esteve at the same time.

One of the two remaining ODESSA killers zeroed in on Rafael Encizo with a blitz of 9 mm Luger slugs. Encizo did not intend to wait around for them. Diving to the floor before any of the Nazi's bullets could connect, the Cuban stretched out his arms as he dropped and let his MP-5 go to work. The ODESSA thug was attempting to correct his aim on his elusive target when the tibia and fibula of both of his legs disintegrated under the onslaught of the 9 mm bone-breakers striking his body.

The gunner went down, collapsing onto his shattered legs, his lowered elevation bringing him into direct contact with a pair of bullets from Encizo's H&K machine pistol. One bullet entered his mouth and continued undaunted out the back of his skull; the other burned a hot hungry hole through the dying man's chest and into his right lung.

The remaining Nazi in the room shrieked at the technicolor reality of the slaughter of his three friends. He wanted no part of it. Raised to believe that being an ODESSA Nazi would lead a charmed life, the frantic thug could decipher nothing charming about the way his companion had died.

The gunner's eyes darted desperately around the lobby, searching for a way out. Anywhere but up the stairs would mean immediate suicide. He triggered a triple-burst of 9 mm hellfire from his MP-40 in the general direction of the lobby's main entrance, then spun on his heels and ran up the steps of the staircase.

Thunder cracked and a bolt of fire tore into the Nazi's side just below his rib cage. His hand clamped over the wound, two of his fingers sinking inside. He moaned, discarding his weapon, and the MP-40 bounced down the steps. The ODESSA gunner lost his balance and slumped to his knees, toppling to his uninjured side. He withdrew his fingers. The uncorked wound bled freely. His mouth yawned wide to scream, but before he could utter a sound his heart quit beating.

Encizo climbed to his feet as Manning rushed to join him. Gunfire reverberated from distant sections of the resort. A faint smell of smoke teased the air.

"Nice bunch," Manning said.

"Real murder when it comes to hospitality," Encizo added.

"What do you say? Stay down here or head upstairs?"

Encizo pointed his thumb to the ceiling.

"Sounds good to me," the Canadian said.

Together the Phoenix Force duo crossed the lobby to the bottom of the stairs. Manning slung his H&K G-3 over his shoulder and brought out his Eagle .357 Magnum.

"Cover me," Manning directed.

"You had the last one," the Cuban reminded him. "This time it's my turn."

"You've got it."

Manning positioned himself at the base of the stairway and Encizo started to climb, taking the steps two at a time. The sound of running feet came from behind the Canadian. Manning whirled, spotting an ODESSA gunman less than fifteen feet away. The Nazi killer was brandishing a 9 mm H&K P-7 pistol.

Gary Manning fired twice, both .357 rockets ripping into the Canadian's flesh-and-blood target like a couple of Magnum piranha. The Nazi's P-7 discharged into the floor as his life drained from his body through the twin holes above his lungs.

Encizo halted long enough to reassure himself that Manning was safe, then continued his race up the steps. An ODESSA Nazi appeared at the top of the stairs—his Beretta 92SB-F hastily aimed in the Cuban's direction. The Phoenix warrior stopped, swinging his MP-5 into play, his mind cursing the fact that he was too slow.

The Beretta fired. Lightning streaked against Encizo's skull. Something warm washed over his eyes. His H&K machine was too heavy to hold. Encizo felt the strength in his legs start to ebb, and then he was falling headfirst down the shaft of a dark bottomless pit.

Manning heard the Beretta's single shot and turned as Encizo's body came tumbling down the steps. A figure moved at the top of the staircase. Manning's hand was a blur of motion as his Eagle flew into battle. Three .357-Magnum meteors took flight. Angry bullets sought flesh and found it. The Beretta dropped from lifeless fingers. One hundred ninety-five pounds of ODESSA garbage crashed to the floor.

Gary Manning crouched and reached for Encizo. The Canadian's fingers checked the side of his friend's neck for a pulse.

David McCarter and François Audouy had also entered the resort, running from the kitchen and through Pic d'Esteve's dining room without being challenged. Tables were set to accommodate approximately thirty diners, but there was nothing to suggest that any meals had been served in the room that evening.

They exited the dining room and moved along a corridor that ran through the middle of the building. The hallway's wooden floors were slick and buffed to a high-gloss shine. Following the corridor around its bend to the right, Audouy informed McCarter, would take them to the lobby.

Multiple gunshots echoed throughout the interior of the resort, but the acoustics in the hallway made it virtually impossible to pinpoint exactly where the distant shots were coming from. Seconds later the gunfire ceased, and McCarter and Audouy continued on their way.

Halfway down the corridor McCarter signaled for Audouy to halt. The British commando cocked his head to the right and listened, his instincts warning him before his hearing did that someone was approaching them from the rear.

"Behind us!" McCarter snapped, spinning in a semicircle and bringing his Ingram MAC-10 around just as two ODESSA Nazis burst into the hallway from the dining room.

"*Scheiss!*" the first Nazi catching sight of McCarter and Audouy exclaimed as he lifted his Spanish CETME Model LC assault rifle to eradicate the intruders trapped in the corridor. His finger wrapped around the Liviano Corto's trigger, but got no farther.

McCarter's Ingram bucked in the Briton's grip as a handful of 9 mm parabellum slugs connected with the ODESSA rifleman. The Phoenix pro was sure no one had ever accused the Nazi gunner of having a colorful personality, but what he lacked in life, he more than made up for in death.

Torn apart with lead from sternum to crotch, the thug's torso belched open like a broken zipper. Blood rained from a half-dozen holes. The Nazi bellowed, then cried like a baby. He turned, falling against the wall, leaving a bright red smear as he slid to the floor.

Audouy's target was a ruthless killer whose weapon was a ready-to-fire MP-40 submachine gun. All the subgunner wanted was for his Nazi comrade to get out of the way so he and his Erna-Herke could fill the narrow corridor with lead. The killer got his wish as the other Nazi left the land of the living disguised as a human paintbrush.

François Audouy took advantage of the same opening, firing a solid stream of 9 mm bullets into the Nazi thug before he could trigger a single shot. The ODESSA gunner grunted. Pink foam sprayed from his mouth and dribbled onto his chin. He suddenly felt tired and wanted to sleep. Again he got his wish.

McCarter pivoted as fresh gunfire erupted from beyond the end of the hallway. Together he and his UCLAT partner ran to investigate.

Yakov Katzenelenbogen and Calvin James had climbed the outdoor staircase to the upstairs balcony. More than a dozen rooms opened onto the balcony. Several doors had been blown off their hinges by the RAG rounds James had fired. Most of the doors were closed. Whatever lay behind them held potential danger for the Israeli and the American.

Katz and James searched the rooms, systematically going from door to door. They moved swiftly, but carefully. Rooms one and two were deserted. The same was true of numbers three and four. They were advancing upon room number five, when a lone ODESSA Nazi stormed through the doorway and made a suicidal charge straight at them.

James and Katz fired simultaneously with their respective SMGs. The American's M-76 and the Israeli colonel's Uzi filled the Nazi with enough heavy metal to stage a rock concert. The thug twitched on invisible strings, dancing with death as bullets thudded into his body and sent him sailing off the side of the balcony.

The muffled report of a handgun came from three doors down. Even as Katz and James recognized the sound for what it was, the unidentified gunman fired again. Both Phoenix Force warriors raced along the balcony to the room in which the shots had been fired. Katz and James took opposite sides of the door. Gently the Israeli commander extended his fingers to test the doorknob.

"It's unlocked!" called a male voice from the other side of the door. "Come inside, Katzenelenbogen! I won't shoot you."

Katz felt the hair along his nape stand on end as his memory successfully matched a face to the owner of the voice. The Israeli shuddered inwardly, and a chill that had nothing to do with the blizzard tripped up his spine. The only face he came up with belonged to a dead man—Adolf Zeigler!

"I'm going in," Katz announced to James.

"You and me both," the black commando stated. "Open 'er up."

Katz turned the doorknob and pushed. The wind took over from there and opened the door with a re-sounding crash. His Uzi held in combat readiness, Katz eased himself around the doorframe and into the room.

"That's better," Zeigler said calmly as Katz entered.

The ODESSA Nazi sat in a chair with his legs crossed. His hands were folded in his lap, a Luger P.O8 gripped in them. A corpse, displaying plenty of brains and little else, was sprawled on the floor at Zeigler's feet.

"Surprised to see your old friend Adolf?" Zeigler inquired, smiling and stroking the barrel of his Luger.

Katz moved to the side as Calvin James entered the room. "I thought you were dead."

"Thanks to you I nearly was," Zeigler said, ignoring James. "But as you can see from the miserable condition of my face, you merely damaged the goods. You started the job, but didn't complete it."

"Not a mistake I'll repeat," Katz promised. "Who is your friend?"

"That is Rottenführer Schmidt. Can you believe it? The fool actually begged me to shoot him so he wouldn't be captured. Given the circumstances under which his request was made, how could I refuse?"

"You're finished, Zeigler. Your idiotic scheme to manipulate the Ocs and put ODESSA on the throne of its own country dies here at Pic d'Esteve tonight."

Zeigler shifted in his seat, but it was not a nervous gesture. The Nazi seemed strangely relaxed and smug under the circumstances. "We shall see," he declared. "You have won the battle, but the war will still be ours."

"Not yours, Zeigler," Katz informed him. "For you, this is the end of the line."

"Not by your hand, Jew," Zeigler said with a twisted smile.

His arm moved, raising the Luger. Katz and James nearly opened fire, but Zeigler did not aim his P.08 pistol at the pair. He abruptly jammed the barrel into his mouth and pulled the trigger. His head smacked against the wall, splashing blood and brain tissue across the surface. Then his body rolled from the chair to the floor.

"Damn," Calvin James muttered.

"Couldn't have happened to a nicer guy," Katz commented dryly.

Katz and James made their way from the room and went downstairs to join the others. A sick feeling of dread washed over them as they finally reached the lobby. McCarter and Audouy moved aside as Katz and James approached.

"What happened?" the Israeli inquired urgently.

Cradling Encizo's bloodied head in his arms, Gary Manning looked up, tears and sadness filling his eyes. "The bastards shot Rafael."

MORE GREAT ACTION COMING SOON

PHOENIX FORCE

#22 Time Bomb

SOUTH AFRICAN TERROR

Phoenix Force, with West German ace
Karl Hahn replacing the disabled Raphael
Encizo, races to South Africa to defuse an
international time bomb whose mechanism has
been triggered by the kidnapping of an anti-
apartheid U.S. senator and a black American
human-rights activist.

Plunged into a dangerous world of intrigue,
racial tensions and terrorist killers, the force
leaves politics to the politicians and comes
in fighting.

MORE GREAT ACTION AVAILABLE NOW

ABLE TEAM

#21 Death Strike

DIE, UNOMUNDO!

Carl Lyons is a prisoner of the Fascist International, and his longtime nemesis Miguel de la Unomundo is offering the Able Team vet an escape from his brain-twisting torture.

The pain was the hammer and the anvil with which Unomundo would smash Lyons until his sanity shattered. And then he would remold the antiterrorist specialist in his own image.

Tortured and terrorized, Carl Lyons is at the mercy of his captor.

Available wherever paperbacks are sold or through Gold Eagle Reader Service. In U.S.A.: 2504 W. Southern Avenue, Tempe, Arizona 85282. In Canada: P.O. Box 2800, Postal Station A, 5170 Yonge Street, Willowdale, Ont. M2N 6J3.

Take
4 explosive books
plus a
mystery bonus
FREE

Mail to **Gold Eagle Reader Service**

In the U.S.
2504 West Southern Ave.
Tempe, AZ 85282

In Canada
P.O. Box 2800, Station A
5170 Yonge St.,
Willowdale, Ont. M2N 6J3

YEAH! Rush me 4 free Gold Eagle novels and my free mystery bonus. Then send me 6 brand-new novels every other month as they come off the presses. Bill me at the low price of $2.25 each— a 10% saving off the retail price. There are no shipping, handling or other hidden costs. There is no minimum number of books I must buy. I can always return a shipment and cancel at any time. Even if I never buy another book from Gold Eagle, the 4 free novels and the mystery bonus are mine to keep forever.

_____

Name   (PLEASE PRINT)

_____

Address   Apt. No.

_____

City   State/Prov.   Zip/Postal Code

_____

Signature (If under 18, parent or guardian must sign)

This offer is limited to one order per household and not valid to present subscribers. Price is subject to change.

166-BPM-BPGE   4E–SUB–1

TAKE 'EM NOW

FOLDING SUNGLASSES
FROM GOLD EAGLE

Mean up your act with these tough, street-smart shades. Practical, too, because they fold 3 times into a handy, zip-up polyurethane pouch that fits neatly into your pocket. Rugged metal frame. Scratch-resistant acrylic lenses. Best of all, they can be yours for only $6.99. **MAIL ORDER TODAY.**

Send your name, address, and zip code, along with a check or money order for just $6.99 + .75¢ for postage and handling (for a total of $7.74) payable to Gold Eagle Reader Service, a division of Worldwide Library. New York and Arizona residents please add applicable sales tax.

Remove from pouch...

unfold once...

unfold twice...

and they're ready to wear.

 GOLD EAGLE In USA:
2504 W. Southern Ave.
Tempe, Arizona
85282

GES1